HARARE NORTH

Brian Chikwava is among the exciting new generation of writers emerging from the African continent. His short story *Seventh Street Alchemy* was awarded the 2004 *Caine Prize* for African Writing. He has been a Charles Pick fellow at the University of East Anglia, and was the recipient of an Arts Council grant in 2005. He lives in London.

D0828814

BRIAN CHIKWAVA

Harare North

VINTAGE BOOKS
London

Published by Vintage 2010

10

Copyright © Brian Chikwava 2009

Brian Chikwava has asserted his right under the Copyright, Designs
and Patents Act 1988 to be identified as the author of this work

First published in Great Britain in 2009 by
Jonathan Cape

Vintage
Random House, 20 Vauxhall Bridge Road,
London SW1V 2SA

www.vintage-books.co.uk

Addresses for companies within The Random House Group Limited
can be found at: www.randomhouse.co.uk/offices.htm

The Random House Group Limited Reg. No. 954009

A CIP catalogue record for this book
is available from the British Library

ISBN 9780099526759

Penguin Random House is committed to a sustainable future for
our business, our readers and our planet. This book is made from
Forest Stewardship Council® certified paper.

Printed and bound in Great Britain by Clays Ltd, St Ives plc

To Mum and Dad, Donna,
Roy, Ronald, Dan, Patience,
Martin, Michael and Godwin

Prologue

Never mind that he manage to keep me well fed for some time, but like many immigrant on whose face fate had drive one large peg and hang tall stories, Shingi had not only become poor bread-winner but he had now turn into big headache for me. When it become clear that our friendship is now big danger to my plan, me I find no reason to continue it, so I finish it off straight and square.

When I climb out of Brixton Tube station that morning, there is white, ice-cold sun hanging in the sky like frozen pizza base. Beyond the station entrance, some chilly wind is blowing piece of Mars bar wrapper diagonal over pedestrian crossing. And the traffic lights – they is red like ketchup.

To the right of station entrance one newspaper vendor stand beside pile of copies of *Evening Standard*. On front page of every one of them papers President Robert Mugabe's face is folded in two. I can still identify His Excellency. The paper say that Zimbabwe has run out toilet paper. That make me imagine how after many times of bum wiping with the ruthless and patriotic *Herald* news-paper, everyone's troubled buttock holes get vex and now turn into likkle red knots. But except for this small complaint from them dark and hairy buttocks, me I don't see what the whole noise is all about.

Outside Lambeth Town Hall I plough through small bunch of mothers in they tracksuits as they dither by the bus stop, blocking the pavement with prams and they large earrings. They give me loud looks.

1

Walking on, I am worryful about what kind of mouth Shingi is going to start throwing around if he ever recover. Although he is still knocked out, maybe when he come around, nightmare will start for me if he start spinning jazz numbers about me. But there is nothing I can do. Me I should not be bothered by none of this.

It don't matter that I am illegal; I have keep his passport because his asylum application get approved by the immigration people some while ago. His passport and National Insurance number come in handy now. His mobile phone too.

His mother back home; she is also part of the problem. She keep writing letters demanding money at each turn. Money for this, money for that, money for everything. The more money I send, only trying to help Shingi out of this situation, the more she behave like he is Governor of Bank of England. Now me I don't want this old hen flapping about over my money like that no more.

And then there is Dave and Jenny, Shingi's homeless friends that have turn the house into some place where there is no break from them slamming doors and people kicking off. Like them immigrants that spend time mixing rhythm and politics under the chestnut tree outside the Ritzy Cinema, Jenny and Dave is also failures in life. They is the first poor white folk that I ever get to know; that is if you don't count the one that live in a drum back home in Harare Gardens. Like them immigrants they also have them asylum-seeker eyes; them eyes with the shine that come about only because of a reptile kind of life, that life of surviving big mutilation in the big city and living inside them holes.

In them months before this day, the day I finish us off straight and square, I can't tell Shingi's mother that Shingi is dying in London because me I see no point in making she cry. My solution has been to send cheerful letters spinning small jazz numbers about Shingi. I also wire she small packets of money and tell she to be patient and all that kind of stuff, you know what it is like when you is trying to keep old hen happy. But look what she do now.

1

No one bother to give me proper tips before I come to England. So on arriving at Gatwick airport I disappoint them immigration people because when I step forward to hand my passport to gum-chewing man sitting behind desk, I mouth the magic word – asylum – and flash toothy grin of friendly African native. They detain me.

Whatever they reasons for detaining me, them immigration people let me go after eight days. I don't grudge them because they is only doing they graft. But my relatives, they show worryful attitude: I have to wait another two days for my cousin's wife to come and fetch me.

The story that I tell the immigration people is tighter than thief's anus. Me I tell them I have been harass by them boys in dark glasses because I am youth member of the opposition party. This is not trying to shame our government in any way, but if you don't spin them smooth jazz numbers then immigration people is never going to give you chance to even sniff first step into Queen's land. That is they style, I have hear.

That it take so long for my cousin and his wife to do anything about me is not good sign. But me I am just happy to get out when the time come.

I am expecting my cousin Paul to come to pick me up from detention centre, but his wife, Sekai, come instead.

I say goodbye to them officers at the reception as I pick my suitcase. Sekai stand some few metres from me, she back straight

4

like that of soldier on parade, and she waist narrower than that of wasp. Dressed neat, hands in she coat's pockets, she keep some distance that is good enough to suggest to them detention people that she really have nothing to do with me but have been forced into situation. She not even bother to shake my hand and only greet me from safe distance and look at my suitcase in funny way. It is one of them old-style cardboard suitcases that Mother have use before I was born and have carry roosters in the past, but it's my suitcase. It still have smell of Mother inside.

Me I don't mind Sekai too much; I was not expect to be welcomed with open arms. Harare township is full of them stories about the misfortunes that people meet; they carry bags full of things and heads that is full of wonders of new life, hustle some passage to Harare North, turn up without notice at some relative's door, only to have they dreams thrown back into they faces. But then again, me I don't think that I am like them people; Paul and Sekai have been given notice that I am soon going to be stepping into they house in east of London.

Sekai lead the way out. We have our first difficult moment when we get to the train station and she expect me to buy my own ticket. That's when it sink inside my head that she have turn into lapsed African, Sekai. Me I am guest and there she is, expecting me to buy my own ticket on the first day? And it's not that me I don't want to buy myself ticket.

'I buy the ticket if I had the money,' I beg she and try to explain.

Me I only have Z$1,000,000 in my bag, which even if I exchange will come to something like £4. The ticket come to £6. Sekai no longer remember who she is or where she come from, I can tell. I am she husband's cousin, have pay for my air ticket but she still expect me to dip into my pocket for train ticket?

'I have no money,' I say, after funny moment when she have hold my gaze and we stand silent investigating each each's face.

Sekai snort in mocking way, roll she eyes and look at me.

In the end she buy the ticket.

Before the end of my first day, I already know that Sekai don't want me to stay with them. But me I really don't want to stay in Harare North too long; I don't want to have vex face all the time because of Sekai. I just want to get myself good graft very quick, work like animal and save heap of money and then bang, me I am on my way back home. Enough pound sterling to equal US$5,000 is all I have to make, then me I'm free man again. I know things is going to get funny if Sekai and Paul start to think that I am real big load on them. But that's how all them people from home behave when they is in Harare North; sometimes you talk to them on the phone asking if they don't mind if you come and live with them and they don't say 'no' because they don't want you to think that they is selfish. They always say '. . . OK, just get visa and come . . .' when they know that the visa is where everyone hit the wall because the British High Commission don't just give visa to any native who think he can flag down jet plane, jump on it and fly off to Harare North, especially when they notice that people get them visitors' visa and then on landing in London they do this style of claim asylum. So people is now getting that old consulate treatment: the person behind the counter window give you the severe look and ask you to bring more of this and that and throw back your papers, and before you even gather them together he have call up the next person. That frighten you and make you feel cheap you don't want to go back again. But it suit all Zimbabweans in Harare North. Even Sekai and Paul; they say yes I can come live with them but now me I know they say that because they was expecting the British High Commission to do the dirty work for them.

I have bring Paul and Sekai small bag of groundnuts from

Zimbabwe; groundnuts that my aunt bring from she rural home. Sekai give the small bag one look and bin it right in front of me. She say I should never have been allow to bring them nuts into the country because maybe they carry disease. Then she go out and buy us McDonald's supper.

Me I am not worried by Sekai's behaviour. But Paul – he seem to have forget how to hit it off with me. We grow up in the same township only some dozen streets from each each so it's not like we is strangers who have been force upon each each by family.

On the day I arrive at they house, Paul come back from graft and only manage to say 'hi' to me before he notice Sekai's pointy eye and disappear into the toilet. When he come out he go into they bedroom. Sekai follow soon after. I never see them again that night so me I watch TV alone and go to bed at midnight. That is maybe the only time I ever watch TV proper in they house. Most of them times the three of us sit in the lounge in funny silence. In less than short time Paul have fall asleep, snoring on the sofa, his mouth wide open.

Sekai go to she night duty at St Thomas' Hospital where she is nurse and Paul start to behave like big nincompoop, being stiff and funny because he is alone with me. He forget he have had bath and run the bath for the second time. What kind of style is this?

Paul don't sit still with me in the lounge. If he come out and tell me straight and square that me living inside they house is making things funny, me I will not hold grudge. That is the proper way to deal with things.

Things will have been better if he had do something about Sekai, like maybe giving she some small baby to keep she busy. But this have not happen since they get married and Sekai know how to play Paul now; most of the time she keep the cold distance between sheself and Paul by sitting at the opposite end of the couch so he don't start getting sexy touches on she. And when the phone ring she pick it up, mute the TV and sit on the couch stroking she dog and chatting to friends for hours. They have wireless phone; she can have go into another room and leave us to watch TV properly, but she don't do that Sekai. She just want me to hear she conversations, especially when she start talking about them Green Bombers, the youth movement boys back home; the boys of the jackal breed. Sekai go on and on about how they is just bunchies of uneducated thugs that like hitting people with sticks. Me I don't say anything as she say all this stuff because I can tell that Sekai don't really know about things going on in Zimbabwe because she have been in England for too long. She buy all the propaganda that she hear from papers and TV in this country. Maybe she think like that because the Green Bombers had visit the village where she grandmother live and the old hen's womb nearly fall out from fright because she have been caught misbehaving, giving food to opposition party supporters.

Green Bombers only look for enemies of the state and Sekai don't understand that because now she and Paul have become some of them people that support Zimbabwe's opposition party. The Green Bombers is there to smoke them enemies of the state out of they corrugated-iron hovels and scatter them across the earth. Sekai and Paul just don't get that, but me I don't say anything and let Sekai yari yari yari on the phone, dissing them Green Bombers. She know nothing. She don't even know Comrade Mugabe. The president can come out to whip you with the truth. Truth is like snake because it is slippery when it move and make people flee in all directions whenever it slither into crowds, but Sekai don't know. Comrade Mugabe is powerful wind; he can blow snake out of tall grass like it is piece of paper – lift it up into

8

wide blue sky for everyone to see. Then when he drop it, people's trousers rip as they scatter to they holes.

Sekai talk too much propaganda on the phone sometimes so me I go inside toilet to sit and think about my old comrade Shingi. He is one of them old friends, you know what it's like with old friends, you know each other so well that sometimes you is not sure if your memories belong to him or vice versa; things can get mixed up and time become one tangled heap and you no longer know whose story belong to who. He is going to be surprised I'm here now. Shingi have arrive in Harare North before me and have already check out things in this city. He already tell me how boring them English girls is because they have fail to appreciate or understand him. Back home, when we was at school, he just run onto the football pitch and kick the ball up as high as he can manage and all the girls go wild cheering, 'Comrade Shingi, Comrade Shingi, the Original Native!' But in England it is different, he complain. One morning while taking walk through park in Brixton he come across group of them girls playing football. When they ball stray towards him he pick it up and hoof it seven miles into the sky but not one cheer come from them girls. They just eye him with small confusion and big fright, which was big shame because Shingi rate it as his best effort ever at kicking ball up high.

In the toilet them memories always start to leap high inside my head and make my head feel like box of frogs. One Saturday morning in our third year at secondary school, Shingi put on brave show that become talk of the year at school. On this freezing Saturday when the air is colder than Satan's nose, one classmate spot him selling bananas at Africa Unity Square. With them temperatures wanting to dive to minus, Shingi is just standing and licking ice lolly and resist everything that the weather throw at him. When news reach school, he become instant hero because he stand his ground in face of winter's dictatorship. 'Yeee, the Original Native, Comrade Shingi is the man.' For one whole term these cries fill the school corridors.

At about the same time, everyone in our class also become aware of how fast Shingi read history textbooks and pick up things with small effort. That is after he submit essay giving big talk on the political philosophy of Mao Tse-tung. He tell how Mao was son of Chinese peasant that live in China, how he was hard worker who was fond of taking cold shower early in the morning. 'Very very very cold shower,' Shingi emphasise, to draw attention to the heart of Mao politic thinking. But when our teacher, Mr Nkabinde, mark the essay, he write 'See me' at bottom of page of Shingi's exercise book.

Now Shingi's deep thinking continue even after he hit Harare North. He have also tell me how he have been investigating another idea that show that under the very quiet face of every Londoner, like them that you see hiding behind they newspapers on trains or buses every morning, the heart of big big traitor is beating; very big traitor that is able rise up against monarch. Shingi say he come to this conclusion after spending very long time checking out them local pubs. That's when he see that there's them names like the King's Head, the King's Arms, the Queen's Head and things like that; evidence of them murdered kings and queens everywhere. What he is still trying to figure out just before I arrive in Harare North is what them English natives have do with the hands and feeties of them dead monarchs for instance. He have also see pub called the Hog's Head and maybe is going to conclude that, in the past, them natives must have get bored clubbing them rulers, and instead turn to swine.

Me I am still sitting in the toilet and now I see things clear: maybe I write letter to President Mugabe and tell him that his troubles with Tony Blair is not as big as he think because if he listen to Shingi's reasoning, then there is good chance that people of this likkle island, with they dislike for them dictators, will soon grab they spades and pitchforks and make short work of Tony Blair when the time come. Pub called Prime Minister's Head is more likely in the future.

I go to bed thinking Shingi. He is big inspiration because if he has come this far there is no reason why me too I cannot make it and make my US$5,000. He have bigger things to deal with. His mother die when he was small and because his mother's sister is not able to have children – some say it's because she have too much beard – the family elders do the ceremony of placing Shingi inside womb of his mother's sister. So he become child of his mother's sister and end up growing with she in Harare.

At the township beer hall, when neighbours have drink too much brew you know how they start throwing around this bad kind of mouth; yari yari yari oh Shingi is totemless child. Oh he don't know his totem. That's because his father is supposed to have been guerrilla before independence and he thief his way into Shingi's mother's knickers during war one night when she visit the village. After that he disappear and no one know anything about him or what happen to him after the war.

And when it's month end and people have get they wages and can now afford bottled beer instead of traditional *chibuku* brew, then it get worse: ah Shingi's father come back from the war disturbed because he spill wrong blood and those bad spirits is avenging now and affect whole family, taking Shingi's real mother away to punish Shingi for sins of his father. Oh yeee bad-luck vibes also slowly getting Shingi's head out of gear. You know that kind of mouth. But all this don't affect Shingi because now he have even make it as far as Harare North and all them beer-mouths is stuck in they hovels in the

11

township bawling they eyes out because price of everything jump up zillion per cent and they can't even afford food or brew now; all them big stomachs gone, they belts is down to they last holes but them trousers is still falling down, big fat cheeks now gone, they heads is thin and overcrowd with teethies. I will tell this to Shingi and he will go kak kak kak kak!

2

Big TV, ready-made meals from supermarket, funny long silences, grunts and making funny faces – that is Paul and Sekai's life. They have been married for ten years. Paul, if he have only once put Sekai through pain of birth, maybe she will have know she place and start to give his relatives the respect that she have to give them.

They also have likkle sausage dog that do *kaka* on the carpet while Sekai cry, 'Sheila, darlin', stop it,' as if this is naughty likkle girl.

Because Paul and Sekai is doing DIY work on they house when I arrive, they sleep me in spare room that is full of MDF boards, bags of plaster, PVC sheets and all. Everyone on the street is doing DIY to they houses, making noise hammering all weekend and sometimes making small neighbour talk with Paul or Sekai as they unload things from they cars.

Paul and Sekai is building small wall across room that I sleep in because they is wanting to make the other half of the room become Paul's study. So when Paul is busy working on the wall I have to help. But that is also because I don't want him to spend too much time alone in the room and end up looking inside my suitcase.

I stop helping Paul when Sekai say my shoes is making the carpet in the house dirty. I go out and sit at the doorstep and start to use screwdriver to pick off the mud that have cake under my boots from walking around outside. But Sekai follow me and ask me to look down on our street and tell she if I see anyone sitting on they doorstep? Me I don't get the score what this is all about until she tell me that this is not township; I should stop embarrass them and start behaving like I am in England.

I turn twenty-two years that day but me I don't tell Paul or Sekai because I know this is wrong place to celebrate birthday. So I go to bed early that evening.

Mother. Home. Early morning. She water bed of tomato plants at the back of house. By doorstep, there is she old shoes. Wet and red with mud.

Mother. She sweep floor. Since she funeral, she have knit sheself back into life. Mother. She expect friends. The kettle on the stove begin to shake lid, letting out steam. Mother throw easy look at it and continue sweeping. Your house is like your head, she say to sheself, you have to keep sweeping it clean if you want to stay sane. She like to say that.

Big fit catch the kettle; it writhe on stove and the lid lift off. Mother sweep on.

There is clink sound at the gate; Mother crane she neck to look out of window. Sibanda the next-door neighbour is returning she bicycle. Mother take kettle from stove and go out to meet Sibanda.

'Wamuka seyi, Sibanda, did you sleep well?' she say, standing outside door. Sibanda have fix bicycle for Mother. He say it was just small puncture. Mother look at she bicycle like, you know what mother is like when she want good job.

'Now I'm old woman I wish I can drive because I don't want to be known as bicycle grandmother,' Mother say and Sibanda laugh.

Now she want to know how much she owe Sibanda but he go all sweet. '. . . ah, not to worry, my sister; I don't buy no spare part this time.'

Mother smile and tell him to write down cost of all them things

14

he have done for she because she have son in Harare North who can pay for all this.

'Don't be too shy to charge him,' she laugh.

Sibanda walk away laughing with hands hold together in front in respectful way. Mother get inside the house and make sheself cup of tea.

Mother start to dust up inside house. In the lounge there is framed photo of me. It stand on the display cabinet looking sweet, being complement by them things inside cabinet: Mother's bestest tea set, and water-glass sets. They is on them white doilies which she have knit all she life. On them glasses is the hens that she knit when she find she have nothing to do. There is half-finished red hen; soon it will be finished and stuffed with cotton wool and put inside display cabinet.

The blue hens in the display cabinet, she throw back into the drawer in the kitchen and the red ones come out. The red hens, Mother's bestest, is same colour as jersey that I am wearing in photograph on she display cabinet. Mother show she friends how to knit them hens over pot of Tanganda Tea. They scribble down them details; wool colour code and all. She dig out the rest of them photos of me in Harare North – me I am feeding them pigeons in this big city. Mother go into show-off style, telling friends yea he is my son that one. Them other women look them photographs; they tea go cold.

'He's my son that one,' Mother continue, but MaKhumalo complain that why am I feeding them pigeons in Harare North when people here is near starving?

They talk talk talk talk like usual until the air crowd up with they voices and me I can't hear nothing now. There is them other sounds in air. Crows. Cries. Over the room me I am like ghost. Outside, black winds start to tear through garden. Lounge window bang and bounce back wide open. Knitting pins drop and go clink clink on cold concrete floor, Tanganda Tea spill everywhere.

15

Silence.

Outside, some big vex whirlwind start. Mother, she leave in big hurry for she bedroom. I find she on she knees pleading with Lord.

I settle over she like mist, Mother.

Mother, I hold she tight in my arms.

'My child,' she cry.

'Mother.'

'My child.'

'Yes, Mother?'

'Mwanangu.'

'Amai.'

Mother. She wrap me up in she arms and hold tight. My small feet lock together, them small toes coil. I'm back in Mother's arms.

'Did you fall, my child?'

I suck thumb and nod. Mother hold me to she bosom and rock me gentle. Then some funny long breast roll out down and swing past my face like pendulum. It come back; dark and dry, it hit my cheek. I miss it. It come back again; now I catch it. Outside, things is now quiet. Inside, breast is cold; the milk dry up long time ago.

I wake up in the morning thinking of Mother. You die and your spirit go into wilderness. One year later, your family have to do *umbuyiso* ceremony to bring your spirit back home so it can leave with other ancestor spirits. Mother, she die of overdose. They carry she to hospital in wheelbarrow and she don't come back. Then they take she body from the township and bury she in rural home under heap of red earth and rocks. Now she spirit is still wandering in the wilderness because family squabbles end up preventing *umbuyiso* and this has not been done for years now. Me I have to go back home and organise *umbuyiso* for she.

I never wanted to leave Zimbabwe and come to this funny place but things force me. I have not even have chance to visit Mother's grave for long time before I come here. And then me I hear that people in the village where Mother is buried will be moved somewhere because government want to take over the area since emeralds have now been discovered there.

I have to keep big focus and soon I'm back home to organise *umbuyiso* for Mother. Even if other family members don't want, I will bring Mother's spirit back from wilderness. But now I have to sit tight and resist jumping into changing my life because of Paul and Sekai or else my plan fall apart and I end up staying in this funny foreign place for ever. Sekai can throw anything she want at me but me I am going to sit tight. Change of life sometimes feel sweet and can give new ginger to your life but sometimes you have to resist it even if you are not favourite pet in the house. Me I know sweet change; I have the same feeling before I join them boys of the jackal breed, the Green Bombers. Those days, nothing is moving in my life because I have just come out of prison and being shoe doctor outside the community hall is not bringing anything no more. And I have just learn that life is not fair. Life make you think that you is frying bean sprouts and then out of nowhere you wake up and find that you is frying wire nails.

If you is back home leading rubbish life and ZANU–PF party offer you job in they youth movement to give you chance to change your life and put big purpose in your life, you don't just sniff at it and walk away when no one else want to give you graft in the country even if you is prepared to become tea boy. Me I know what I have to do when the boys come to take me in they van: the people's shoes, broken belts and all that kind of stuff, I toss them out onto pavement, give my stall one kick and it fall over easy. That's it! Me I jump onto the van as it speed off. I'm free. That's how new beginnings start. My life have found big and proper purpose. Those was the days. New life booming inside your head. You love the life, you like Tom the driver and you love the van because Tom call it the jackal. Chenhamo 'Original Sufferhead' is hanging and swinging from the van's door waving ZANU–PF party flag and defying the whole township as you speed away into another life. And the jackal – it is full with them new boy recruits heading for training camp; they is all lugging football-size eyes because they don't know what everyone who remain behind is going to think of them now, but me I don't let such foolishness hassle me. I like this. Tom is putting his foot down giving the jackal more fire and threading his way through them traffic lanes, trying to put himself in good position for when the traffic lights turn green. Everything feel alive. Other drivers flee out of the lanes. Original Sufferhead curl his lip over his broken tooth and let out one shrieking sound that make the hair on your back stand. Then he shout: 'Keep foot down on the juice, Tom, if anything happen we is there to witness everything for you if police ask questions!'

The jackal is jumping crazy across them lanes; other drivers don't know what to do. They push down on they horns with frightened faces as the jackal advance. Yes, those was the days.

US$5,000 – US$1,000 for my uncle because that's what I owe him for my plane ticket here, and US$4,000 to sweet that pack of them hyenas that chase me around Zimbabwe wanting to catch me until I have to run away here because I don't have the money that they want so they can make my troubles go away.

That's what Comrade Mhiripiri tell me and he is trustful man. US$4,000. He is commander of them boys of the jackal breed and is the first big man that you meet on the first day you arrive at training camp. Before you have even manage to jump out of the jackal Comrade Mhiripiri is barking and barking and marching around the jackal holding his hands behind and pointing his long beard up at every problem that he see on the face of every new recruit: you why you wearing earrings like you is woman, you why you walk like old man, you why you shave your head like you come from Apostolic Faith sect, yari yari yari. That's his style, Comrade Mhiripiri. He make everyone scatter scatter quick; no one want to be under his eye because soon his beard is pointing at you. But he have no doubt about the straightness of our path and he don't allow them bookish doubts to worry him. For traitors punishment is the best forgiveness, that's what he say. And it is because of giving forgiveness that my troubles start. Them enemies of the state was on the loose, waving opposition party flags from behind every small bush that Comrade Mhiripiri's beard is pointing at. That was when we visit Goromonzi.

After Comrade Mhiripiri have tell us to take one traitor by force from Goromonzi police hands we take him to them tall trees. Comrade Mhiripiri have ask me to lead them boys on account of me I know heaps of history.

This opposition party supporter, he have been arrest on account of he is one of them people that attack our party's supporters who have invade white man's farm. When we get to them tall trees we only ask him why they attack the sons and daughters of the soil, but the traitor say the soil belong to the white man and that our brothers and sisters is invaders. Me I give him one small lesson in history of Zimbabwe – how in the 1890s them British fat stomachs grab our land, pegging farms by riding horse until it drop dead; that just mark only one side of the farm boundary and that's where the corner peg go. But even after this, the traitor, who have been farm labour supervisor all his life and now have barrel stomach that is so taut any blunt old instrument can punch through it easy if that become necessary, he is still saying that the farmer buy the land. How do you say you buy land that was never sold by no one in the first place unless you like buying things that have been thief from someone? 'What kind of style is that?' me I ask him and he start filling us to the brim with gallons of bookish

19

falsehoods that is stronger than overproof brandy and of course that get us drunk and soon we start dancing around him and singing revolutionary songs. By the time we is sober and staggering all over with big hangover the police is crawling all over me and Original Sufferhead. 'We give him one heap of forgiveness and can't remember nothing at all about what happen because he get us so drunk,' me I tell the police, but they don't want to believe. The winds is blowing through the nation and making trees swing in every direction but the police only want to know how one leaf fall from tree. What kind of style is that? Because of life of one traitor?

When they give us bail me I have to run back to Harare without even see Comrade Mhiripiri. By now I know that the police is full of traitors that want to protect them enemies of the state. Soon they start telling Comrade Mhiripiri that for US$1,000 they can make my docket disappear. If that happen the court can't do nothing and soon my troubles go away. Comrade Mhiripiri keep sending text messages to my phone: yeee them police people is saying this, yeee they is saying that; yeee now they is wanting more. I'm flapping my ears every direction trying to hear where I can borrow money; my uncle promise to help me and before he have even get it Comrade Mhiripiri is saying they now want US$2,000 and before I know it all kind of hyena policemen and magistrates is crawling all over my case wanting they cut and now I have to find total of US$4,000 to buy my freedom.

Now me I am jumping around to try to put money together and suddenly Comrade Mhiripiri stop sending messages. I try to call him to hear what the score is but his phone is no more contactable. Then Tom start sending text messages that don't make no sense; yeee the police is now after Comrade Mhiripiri; yeeeeeee he have run away to UK. 'This is not good sign,' my uncle say. I don't want to leave the country because I have not visit Mother in two years. But I have to go because me I know what Chikurubi Maximum Prison is like; I have been there before and it is full of them people that carry likkle horrors such as them sharpened bicycle spokes and they want you to donate your buttocks so they can give you Aids; if you refuse then bicycle spoke go through your stomach like it is made of toilet paper and you is bleeding inside all night and have no chance of making it to the morning. No one can want to go there again. Life is not fair me I know after they hold the spoke to my heart.

But right now me I sit tight because there is no reason going back home if you can't buy your freedom from them those hyenas. Even if Sekai think that me I am *mamhepo* – the winds; them bad spirits – I keep the discipline and try not to end up burying Paul and she under the bathroom floor.

3

'You have to behave and watch what you say to people,' Sekai say. She have cook heap of food and have invite heap of she friends from work to come and eat in this evening. Two doctors have just arrive; one is white man with funny accent and another one I don't hear where he is from but he is Nigerian. Paul get them beer, and start talk talk to them in lounge while I sit quiet in corner of room watching TV because Chelsea is playing Arsenal. Sekai don't want me to talk to them visitors because she think I end up embarrassing them, I know.

Small group of them five nurses also arrive; they is from home and all over Africa. Me I go and lie down in my room but Paul call me so I can come and meet them nurses. He even give me one can of beer and say I should sit in lounge with everyone.

Yakov, the Russian doctor, start talk to me. 'Traitors is very hard to kill,' I start telling him. 'That is why Grigori Rasputin was still fighting back even after he have been given enough cyanide to kill ten horses, shot many times and thrown into ice-cold river.' Russians was our comrades because before independence them guerrillas used to leave Zimbabwe to be trained in Russia. I don't know if Yakov know.

Sekai, who is busy putting food on the table now, shoot out of room calling me to follow she to the kitchen. When I get to the kitchen she give me money and tell me to go buy more beer from corner shop. There's heaps of beer and wine in the fridge and she still want more?

I come back from buying beer and everyone is already sitting at table and eating. There is no more chair for me to sit at table so I have to take my plate of food and sit on couch and eat quiet. Because I'm not talking to no one me I go to my room after eating.

Sekai come to check things in my room when she hear she sausage dog crying. It was lying on my bed, me I tell she.

'They say you are not entitled to get weekly benefit because you are our dependant,' Paul say as he put the phone down. That's because this morning there is letter that arrive for me from them immigration people talking about what I am allowed and not allowed to do in England. Paul give them phone call. Now it turn out I am not allowed to work until my asylum get approved. And I'm not even allowed benefit money. People say asylum sometimes take years to get approve.

'Do you know what happen to things like people's graves when government takes over the area for mining?' I change subject now and ask Paul. He have degree in rural and urban planning. He just stare into the distance. I sniff sniff that he don't want to talk about this because last week Sekai have already say what is happening in Mother's village is because people like me have been supporting corrupt government. Now that emeralds have been discovered there we will soon hear that the area has been take over by some minister's company, that's what Sekai say.

Shingi; I don't want to make worryful situation for him. I don't want to hang my problems around his neck. At school he have habit of disappearing when he get upset or don't like something but can't tell you straight and square. Me I don't want situation where I bring my problems to him and he hide from me. No one like people with problems.

I don't have Shingi's address or phone number. But I have his email address.

Paul and Sekai's computer have Internet but I don't even try to touch it.

'Are you looking for graft?' Paul ask me. He know that me I am not supposed to look for job but now he say I can maybe try to find graft but I have to be careful because if they catch me, that's the end of me. I don't know if Paul trying to set me up or what. He even say I can use they Internet if I want although he don't think Internet will have jobs for people that have no work permit.

'Feel free to use Internet,' he say. Me I nod and play like I am dumb native who have no self-motivate, even when I know that if I lay my finger on computer without permission, Sekai is going to put my arse in bin bag and throw it onto next flight back home.

Because Sekai is still out on night duty, Paul even show me how to use they Internet and what not to do.

Immigrant people's contribution to this country is equal to one Mars bar in every citizen's pocket every year. That's the first story I read when I start interneting. Sekai is busy putting Mars bars in other people's pockets but can jump on she relative if he touch she bread. That's Harare North for you.

I spend tons of days interneting for graft when Sekai is not around but me I can't find no graft. There is nothing on Internet for someone who want to swing the hammer or pickaxe or push the broom.

I send message to Shingi greeting him and wishing him well. I don't hear from him so I spend long time wondering if he is too busy.

After weeks I hear from Shingi, telling me about how he have been too busy and have just move to Brixton and how he is now

24

living in shared house with Aleck, someone that he have been connect to by Zimbabwean old man who recently start living in Brixton after running away from Zimbabwe because the police was after him. He is busy because now he is starting new graft with landscaping company in Wimbledon and his asylum application have been approve very fast. Asylum take years to get approve but his get approve in matter of months.

Shingi is excite to hear from me and I tell him that he have not see nothing yet because soon, once I have settle in Harare North, me I can catch for him heaps of them London girls with they pointy shoes and sexy skirt. Shingi go kak kak kak kak.

Shingi tell where he is now living and say it's OK if I come to visit him on Friday evening when he is back from his new graft. If he is not home I will find girl called Tsitsi to let me into they house; she is always home.

Last month Paul give me £20 so I can use for transport if I have to travel and look for graft. That's what I take out of my suitcase and put inside my pocket.

I don't want to spend most of Friday inside Paul and Sekai's house; it's better to spend day checking out Brixton and then meet Shingi in the evening.

On Thursday evening I tell Paul that some friend from home want to put me on right road to graft so I have to go to Brixton early in morning but I have not travel on London Underground on my own before. If I get lost somewhere Paul and Sekai is maybe going to have big party and not bother look for me.

Paul now want to be extra helpful to help me get to Brixton. In the morning, on his way to graft, he come with me on Central Line, and at Oxford Circus, he even take me to platform for Victoria Line that go to Brixton. I know he is trying to help me find the way out of they life, old Paul.

On the train to Brixton I am wondering if Shingi have change since he come to London. Even at primary school he make me laugh when we play in the playground. But is he still also shy boy? One day during break time at school me I am on my own standing on the edge of the fishpond near the school playground eating my bread and looking at them fish that look like carrots. Shingi join me because everyone in class is still new and Shingi don't really have friends yet. I don't see him creeping up on me; the first thing I see is his reflection on surface of water in the fishpond. When our eyes clash, he get shy and soon disappear. I never talk to him again until the second term. By then Shingi have become the butt end of every joke in class because he have glasses that is so thick when he blink it look like two big butterflies have flutter they wings behind his glasses. Then one day the boy that sit next to Shingi want to put him in one big fix and shout at the top of his voice that Shingi have said that he want to fry Thoko in Olivine cooking oil. Now, Thoko is this big girl that sit in the front row in classroom and sometimes she come to school smelling of Olivine cooking oil because sometimes that's what she use because she mother cannot afford Vaseline. She have already take on two boys since beginning of the year because they make fun of she by saying she is ready to be fry. She mop the floor with them and make them look cheap.

Now Shingi spend rest of the day in class cowering at the back of classroom saying he never say he want to fry anyone. But Thoko have already make announcement that she want to straighten him up after school.

After school everyone looking forward to another fight and rush to the school gate to join Thoko and wait for Shingi. Shingi hide in the toilet and not come out. Everyone wait and wait but Shingi stay put inside toilet. Then after long time he uncoil himself and step out of toilet and out of school yard thinking that everyone have give up now, only to find Thoko and everyone further down the road under *marula* tree where everyone is eating *marula* fruit and waiting. Now, Shingi can't run back because it's too late. He deny everything – he deny that he have been hiding in toilet or that he said he want to fry Thoko. He even almost deny that his name is Shingi. But Thoko just want to show him what she can do. She have put she school bag down on the edge of the dusty road and have tuck she dress into she knickers' elastic hem-band like them girls do when they is playing netball. And as is usual with them fights, other classmates have rush to make them two sand breasts in the middle of the path. One stand for Shingi's mother's breast and the other stand for Thoko's mother's breast. To make challenge Thoko kick Shingi's mother's breast into the air in that style, you know, like your mother's breast is rubbish. Now, Shingi is lugging eyes like thief that has just been catch, and without any way to frighten she, he kick Thoko's mother's breast, but he don't flatten it out because he don't want to get Thoko more vex. The fight now start and Shingi almost fainting. He throw half-dozen weak punches before Thoko land one clean cracking slap on his face and Shingi's glasses fly into the air. Now with bad vision, Shingi throw another bad effort. Thoko land another one on the other eye. That's when Shingi bawl for his mother: *Maiwe Amai! Mama, Mamaa!* I have to pick his glasses and give them to him while everyone piss they pants laughing. That's the first time I ever accompany him home. Me I tell him that next time someone want to fight him he should pick rocks, hit they head and chase them away.

At Brixton station people is leaping into my face from every direction. None of them talk to each each. They is just pushing faces into mine and walking. They don't smile.

I spend the day wandering around just looking at Brixton, them shops and the market that is so busy it feel like you have stick your head inside anthill. By afternoon I am bored and hungry so me I go sit on bench at bus stop and take out of my pocket the A–Z map that Paul lend me. Shingi don't live far from here.

4

It look like one heap of bricks that stand out from other houses because of its grey brick. That's the house where Shingi live. It have two top windows that have red brick arch. That make the windows look like big sad eyes. Below them sad eyes there is one large bay window that stick out like nose. When I look at the nose, the eyes and black parapet wall – this is Shingi straight and square. But you don't tell anyone that they head look like house if you still want to be friends.

So, Shingi live inside this head?

Tsitsi fling the door open when I knock. She is small girl with sharp look in she eye, nose as small as chicken poo dropping and face drawn tight over small skull. She have the fizzy behaviour of Coca-Cola drink but maybe it's she own kind of rural behaviour because she come from small village in Mashonaland East Province.

She have just turn seventeen she say without me asking.

She wear red-on-white polka-dot dress, one side slipping off she shoulder so the dress hang on she like scarecrow's drapes. She is also wearing yellow-flower headscarf on she head; tied twice over around she head, knotted first at the back and then at the front. She bite bottom lip like she is shy. She have one dimple on one cheek.

Across she left cheek, the tail of one long thin scar maybe caused by snapping barbed wire, break in two as it jump over she left eye and start again above eyebrow before fading out on forehead. She eye have survive.

She take me to the kitchen and the air smell of bad cooking and the sink have one heap of dirty dishes and all. It's like they lie there for donkey years. The ceiling on one corner is growing mushrooms and things.

Rule No. 1: DON'T eat what you did not buy!
Rule No. 2: DON'T eat what you did not buy!
Rule No. 3: DON'T eat what is not yours!
Rule No. 4: If you don't work you don't eat.
Rule No. 5: Wash your pots and plates after eating, your
            mother is not here to wash them for you!

That's them house rules on piece of paper that is stuck onto kitchen door. I have not finish reading all of them and Tsitsi already have got she hand over she mouth like she is trying to stop laughter coming out. Like I am visitor who was not supposed to have see this rudeness.

She start cracking knuckles of she fingers with embarrassed smile and lead me out of kitchen.

Shingi sleeps in the lounge; he share the room with Farayi. Two mattresses is on rotting floorboards, blankets all over, small heaps of things telling one story of big journey that is caused by them dreams that start far away in them townships. I can sniff sniff them natives' lives squatting under the low damp ceiling like thieves that have just been catch.

Tsitsi is small girl and now being taken care of by Aleck who feel sorry for she, Shingi have tell me. She have run away from tyrant auntie who is married to doctor, so she say, and Shingi also tell me how she visa have now expire. Me I have hear this number before; like them other stories that come from abroad, it has been tell many times in townships: some poor relative is lift out of poverty and is taken to them big lights of foreign city, is made to babysit, cook great mountains of meals, make she hosts' bed every morning, even touching them things that should have been taboo for she to even see – things like the father of the house's underwear that is full of them skid marks. Soon this get father of the house's head all out of gear and he start wondering what else this hard-working thing can provide. It don't trouble him with clever argument like the wife do, and it is easy with everything he ask for. That always ends with the usual number playing: family scandal, disgraced man and, sometimes, unwanted baby.

As soon as she have show me around the house Tsitsi throw sheself into inside cupboard, come out with can of sardines, and wasting no time, open it, pour it onto small plate and give it to me to eat. Then she heave she small skeleton onto the cupboard top, sit cross-legged, leaving me abandoned on the kitchen floor.

She ask where I get them from, pointing at them my glasses.

I don't want to tell she to heat them sardines for me.

'You want bread?' She eyes bulge in they sockets like she head have just been hit by big idea. She head is cocked, one ear in front. She is expecting answer. Now I am not hungry.

She head jump jump on she neck as she look at me, this small funny rural girl that want me to eat cold sardines.

I put my plate of them sardines on cupboard and walk to the sink, pick empty water glass. The glass slip off my hand and come crashing on the edge of the sink bowl; it break and fill the kitchen with the kind of fright that fill the room when you have break your mother's bestest teapot. I look at Tsitsi and she hand is over she mouth like I have commit big crime.

I go down on floor picking up them glass pieces. Tsitsi jump off the cupboard and run to get broom and dustpan from behind the kitchen door.

'It's OK, don't worry,' she laugh. 'It's Farayi's glass.' She start to sweep glass from floor and I am just standing there. I pick my plate of sardines again to give my hands something to do. I put one sardine piece inside my mouth.

From upstairs, some baby start to cry. Tsitsi drop everything and run to she room upstairs. She run back down with the baby.

'I've bring you one big comrade,' she say standing by kitchen door. This is the baby that she have been telling me about. It's because of the baby that she say she have to go back to she aunt but she is too scared to go by sheself and want Aleck to accompany she.

I have finish picking them glass so I follow she into lounge. She go to Shingi's bed. She tiny skeleton fold neat as she sit on the bed, crossing she legs and holding the baby close to she bosom. With one hand she pull she blouse up. She don't wear bra; she left breast jump out and hang like talisman. It look bigger than the other. She bring she baby closer, bending she back. Baby catch it like thief. I stand leaning against the wall watching.

When she have finish feeding the baby she unfold she legs. As she get onto she feet, there is sound of ripping cloth. She turn around to look and there is one clean new slit running down she dress, from she bum all the way down and through hemline. Behind she, poking out of the mattress there is short rusty wire.

As if nothing has happen, she put the baby on the bed, get up, pick he and start talking motherly gibberish to him. Then she turn to me and tell me to hold baby and help she put him on she back.

I take the baby, hold him as she fall down on she hands and knees in front of me.

'Put him on my back.'

I step towards she, and place him on she back, flat on his stomach.

Tsitsi want the shawl; I grab it from the mattress, stretch it out and put it on so it hang both sides even. Tsitsi move she back up slightly, holding it horizontal as she grab them two ends of the shawl hanging on both sides of she torso. She pull them two ends down and across she ribcage where she hold them together with one hand while she stretch other hand out to tuck the shawl under the baby's bottom. She jerk baby up and begin to tie the two ends together. Then she stand up. With both hands holding together behind she, cupping baby bottom, she start to shake baby gently, shaking she back gently. Then she break into lullaby, and with she head leaning to one side she look like real mother.

Ru ru mwana
Ru ru mwana
Mwana arikuchema
Arikuchemerei?
Arikuchemera bota
Bota nderani?
Nderekacheche
Kacheche karipi?

Shingi is still not home and here in the kitchen Farayi is throwing heap of stories at me.

'I was teacher at mission school,' he say. You can tell straight away he is that kind of boy that don't break wind even under them blankets because that's where he do most of his prayers. He is the one that share room with Shingi and have live with Aleck from the beginning and know everything about who have live in the house before and have been telling me how he run away from his school where he was teaching religious education. He also have bum that bounce about inside his trousers in disorganised way like bunch of firewood that has not been tie properly.

Without asking, I already know that he have graft at Tooting where recruitment agency put him to do photocopying and stationery for NHS. He juggle it with another graft at some fried chicken takeaway. His papers is not in order; he have do that style of getting visitor's visa and then stepping off with big plan to go back home on the 44th of the month. That's a more direct way; many people do that style because other ways is complicated. Like the Commonwealth visa thing I hear about before I come; they give you two years if you is under twenty-eight years. But you have to wait for months and me I have no time to do it. Also they want you to show that you have truck-load of money before they give you visa because if you is poor then you end up desperate and start taking them Mars bars out of local people's pockets when you is supposed to put them inside.

Farayi talk talk talk.

'You talk too much,' me I tell him straight and square and he get the score.

Aleck arrive from his job and the moment he walk into the house Tsitsi and Farayi is on good behaviour. Tsitsi stop giggling too much and Farayi tie his bundle of firewood tight.

Aleck have the high head of someone that is used to giving orders and the sharp eyes of grown-up school head boy; someone that have perfect the style of squinting his eyes before making them quick and hard judgements. I greet him like any other *blazo* when he come into the kitchen. He smile. One of them tight smiles that Londoners flash at you and leave you not sure

34

if they want to smile at you or if they have change they mind.

He pick cup and walk to sink to drink water. It's his step that tell everything – here is head boy that has turn into proud hard man as he take on the world and take stranded likkle girls like Tsitsi under his wing. Many Zimbabweans in London only care for they stomachs and will never do that kind of thing. Maybe he was also Boy Scout.

After getting bread out of his bag and putting it in cupboard, Aleck head upstairs to his room.

Shingi appear just when me I am thinking that I should go back to Paul and Sekai. I'm with Tsitsi in the kitchen. He is very hard to recognise after such long. His boots is covered with mud. Looking through his thick-rim owl glasses he blink in funny way when he see me. Whatever Harare North have do to him, I have no way to tell. At the bottom of his glasses' left lens, one crack that once try to scream out in all directions is lying frozen and all them glass fragments holding in place.

At first we don't know what to say to each each. Then he smile and prod prod me with his stump finger in that playful way of his; that is his way of show fondness because Shingi don't do hugs. It feel funny when he stab stab you with his stump finger. They have to cut Shingi's finger at hospital after he get bite by puff adder at school. That's why he have stump.

The meal that Shingi cook me is the wickedest. He is in good form because he is happy I'm here. Soon we is alone in the kitchen and the comrade is laughing and telling me food jokes about what I should eat when I'm in Harare North.

He also tell me not to worry about Paul and Sekai; I can sleep here tonight.

We can share my bed, Shingi say. Now he tell me about how he always go trawling through them neighbourhood's bins and skips finding good things that wasteful Londoners throw away.

Most of them things you can fix if they is not already in perfect working order, Shingi say with big ginger. That's how he find his mattress.

All evening Shingi is in form. Everyone in the house is feeling intimidate by our loud friendship – big laughs, banging of kitchen cupboards and clanking of pans as Shingi wash things. Tsitsi and Aleck who have one room each upstairs stop coming out now. Farayi is in they room, keeping to his corner since I tell him that he talk too much.

Then Aleck come down with headmaster kind of face and tell us to keep the noise down.

When we start eating the *sadza* and stew that Shingi have cook, we have already whip each each into big happiness and end up doing some old food game that we play years ago at school. But we have to whisper to each each so others don't get disturbed. The game – you have two chances to guess the original source where the food come from and if you fail then the other person possess you and can order you to bring him food for morning break period until he fail to make right guess.

Food have always been our game. It is also source of trouble. And the reason Shingi always lose the game at school is because me I always know where the food he bring is coming from. That's because when we is ten, I discover everything about the food habits at his home. It happen when we come back from school with Chamu. Chamu have just become Shingi's new stepbrother in funny way because Shingi's second mother have now decide to get married for second time to bus conductor who have already move in. The conductor don't want to make more babies because he have his son Chamu and is only interested in front bum – that's the kind of mouth the whole township throw around. Me I am in habit of leaving Shingi and his new brother at they doorstep because Shingi's mother, MaiShingi, don't like me because I make Chamu and Shingi do mischief. But one day, because MaiShingi have gone somewhere, Shingi take me inside they ground-floor flat to hang out. And then Chamu discover that his mother have forget to lock the door to she bedroom.

We go into bedroom and go straight for them stockpiles of food that MaiShingi have hide under she bed before she go out because she fear them boys' appetite in she absence. Condensed milk, sugar, bread, margarine, Mazoe orange drink – all is up for grabs. After big feast, we turn our attention to the *sadza* and okra that MaiShingi have leave for Chamu and Shingi on the coal stove in the kitchen. Later we rub our swelled stomachs and go kak kak kak.

But when MaiShingi discover that she bedroom have been raid she get super vex, telling Shingi he should write letter to his uncle Sinyoro and tell him that he is living large here, being keep well fed and is also busy thiefing from she. Sinyoro was MaiShingi's big brother and the one that take care of Shingi's school fees because he was schoolteacher and have lot of money.

Then she turn to Chamu and bury him under with heap of them words: yari yari yari I don't know where this come from, it is not from your father's side of family and also not from your mother's side because even if she was shebeen queen, she never thief one single cent from anyone.

She end by threaten to kick both of them out of she house. All this heap of trouble after she have straighten them out with long piece of sugar cane.

From then on, every time Shingi bring food to school, me I only have to say it come from under his mother's bed and Shingi most of the time have lose the food game. I possess him. I still possess him.

5

Sekai give me hard time about where I have been. I tell her that I decide to sleep over at friend's house because he promise to find me job but she keep going on yari yari saying don't I know that I am not allowed to work in this country. And Paul don't say nothing even if he is the one that tell me to look for graft.

'Is there somewhere secret that you are stashing the bread because I don't understand how since you arrive it disappear so fast?' Sekai ask me when things have calm down. Now this style of sliding tackle that she is tearing into me with, me I don't know what to do with it. If I find graft and start making money, me I can sniff sniff that she is going to report me to immigration people. And if she don't do that, then she is going to start charging me big rent and food money and I will spend all my life working to pay rent and will never be able to go back.

On Monday evening Paul is still not back from his graft by nine o'clock and Sekai now go to night duty leaving the phone unlocked. I tell Shingi the whole story and the kind of style that Sekai playing on me here and how she give me hard time because I don't sleep in they house on Friday night. And Paul don't even say anything as if he have nothing to do with it. Shingi just going kak kak kak and say that's the reason he move out of his cousin's house; things get funny and air in the house fill-up with of funny silences.

I have not even ask him and Shingi say that if I want graft

maybe I can try the company that he know in Wimbledon because they is looking for more labour; they don't make big deal if your papers is not OK. Now I am full of big cheer. Me I just want to find my money and then boom, I disappear, I tell him.

Last year, before I leave Zimbabwe, if you wanted US$5,000 you have to find £2,777.78. The exchange rate was 1.80. Last week it stand at 1.89. Maybe in few months exchange rate jump to 2.5.

I get the graft on the spot but because I don't have no safety boots, they say it is best if I start when I have buy pair of boots. That is because they rules say 'no safety boots, no job'. On the way back home, now me I see that I have one fat problem staring straight into my face: Sekai is going to sell me out to them immigration people, I know. She have not tell me nothing but after reasoning hard me I can hear it loud and clear inside my head what she want to do.

I talk to Shingi about this trick problem. Me I have not even ask for anything and he say he is going to talk to Aleck. Aleck will have to hit me £25 per week for rent, Shingi tell me after talking to Aleck. Me I don't mind as long as he don't take away all my money and I end up working in this country for ever.

In the morning I am alone inside the house; Paul have gone to work very early and Sekai not yet back from night shift at St Thomas' Hospital. She usually crawl in at about 10am, so inside the house it's quiet.

I know that Sekai is not so hot on me coasting around in they house during the day, eating they bread and eggs. Even if I am happy to have new graft, I have not forgot the kind of mouth she been throwing around in them past weeks. At one time before I learn that I am not allowed to work, me I tell she that I don't know where to start to look for graft. Yari yari yari yea when people is in Zimbabwe they fill the air with cries saying they want to come to the big lights but once they is here you find them blinking like lost goats, that's what she say to me. That make me disappear into the toilet and close the door behind me with big force on that day. Even while inside toilet I hear she talking to Paul about how, like many of them Zimbabweans who don't know what else to do in the UK, I am only going to end up becoming one of them BBCs – British Buttock Cleaners – looking after old people that poo they pants every hour. She also say she think that my uncle should not have buy me plane ticket so I can run away from the police in Zimbabwe. I should have just face trial, that's the kind of mouth she throw around.

Me I can stand anything that Sekai throw at me if I want but this morning when I remember that only some few days ago she have even say President Mugabe is stubborn old donkey and will chase away all rural people from they villages if he can find emeralds or diamonds there, me I get out of bed, pack my bag, kick sausage dog out of my way and go down to the garage to buy gallon of petrol for them. The sofas, beds, sausage dog – I want to soak everything. I have already pack my suitcase and I am thinking whether to start with lounge or they bedroom when I remember that they is my relatives and that old Paul help me get to Brixton. So without doing nothing, me I drag my suitcase out of they house.

When I am halfway down the street I remember that them streets in that area is always full of dog *kaka*. So I go back to the house and get the big screwdriver that Paul use for DIY. I need something to scrape it off in case I have accident and step on dog *kaka*.

Aleck have small small hands but he have been in London for four years and is the guru and big man in the house. He is shop assistant in Croydon but can point them places if you want something; he know which is best markets to buy clothes from and also know many Zimbabwean contacts if you want to send things back home. He is also the one that point Shingi in right direction so he get graft in Wimbledon.

First day in the house – Aleck come from his graft in the evening and go straight to his room upstairs without saying nothing to me, Shingi, Tsitsi and Farayi as we talk in the kitchen. After half-hour he call me to his room. It's like those days at school when headmaster call you to his office.

He is lying on his bed, you know like tired big tycoon, and is busy sending messages on mobile phone. There's Nike shoes and shirts in disorder all over floor of his room and pictures of people that play for Arsenal on the wall opposite his bed. And one picture of him, all alone on the other wall and looking square at them Arsenal football players like they belong to him. Chelsea is better team.

He is busy smiling to himself and sending messages and keep me waiting so me I stand there not knowing what to do with my hands. I can't even walk because I will make noise on them floorboards because I am wearing them safety boots that Shingi have buy for me today since I promise I will pay him back when I get paid.

When he finally finish sending them messages Aleck throw his phone down on bed with pretend carelessness.

'Right,' he say to himself as he sit up on his bed and lean against wall to show that now is time for serious talk. He start by telling me about them house rules that is on kitchen door and then go on to talk other things; that we have to clean up so the house don't get dirty. That I can find mattress for myself in the skips. Shingi have already say it's OK for me to share his bed until I find mattress.

*   *   *

42

The first thing you should know when you live in Harare North: if people tell you something cost X, remember to allow 25 per cent for them things that have been hide. Rent is supposed to be £25 per week; Aleck say that's true but we have to add another £5 per week for the electricity and gas to make £30 per week.

Another thing: always push for them more favours because if you don't then you don't get nothing. Aleck say he is going to be nice to me and give me soft landing by not charging me any rent for this week because we is already in the middle of it. I ask him if he maybe also give me soft landing for next week because me I am still new native in town and need more time to find my feeties; he don't answer but scratch his jaw slow to show that he is reasoning about it.

By the time we hit the weekend he have tell me it's OK if I take another week of soft landing. This is big scoop, even if Aleck tell me this with voice that sound like he is mourning this decision. Before Aleck agree I have been asking Shingi to push Aleck for me but he say that he have use up all his favours for this week because he have ask Aleck for too many things. We don't want to use them up all our favours all the time or else something big happen that require us to use favours and if we have use them all then we is in trouble, Shingi warn me. But if I had listen to him I would have end up snoozing and losing.

The third thing: never listen too much to propaganda from people like Sekai telling you that your mother's village is going to be take over by mining company that belong to some minister. You always know more than you believe in but always choose what you believe in over what you know because what you know can be so big that sometimes it is useless weapon, you cannot wield it proper and, when you try, it can get your head out of gear and stop you focusing. Soon you lose the game and end up dying beyond your means in Harare North, leaving behind debts and shabby clothes. I have hear all these kind of stories.

You see now I was right to ask for soft landing, I tell Shingi. He don't say nothing; the week has end and now Aleck have give me more soft-landing time. Also, after three days of working in Wimbledon I have now been paid my wages but for funny reason the company that we graft for have put me on emergency tax code and thief away heaps of my money; the money that I get paid all go to Shingi to pay for the boots that he buy me. Me I explain to Shingi how this emergency tax code thing is big con because that's too many Mars bars already.

On Saturday morning we is still lying in bed and this Zimbabwean woman called MaiMusindo come to our house. She is big woman with small head, hard-bitten face and tongue that is like old shoe leather. She have been in England for maybe twenty years and come to our house on the morning of my first Saturday there. She work at the African hair salon with them Ghanaian, Nigerian and Kenyan women who is also specialists in all styles. It's them salon woman that provide midwife help in the salon back room when Tsitsi give birth to she baby.

MaiMusindo is frightful woman. Before she arrive Aleck and Tsitsi have been restless, running up and down the stairs getting ready.

MaiMusindo used to be spirit medium; she still do rituals and is in touch with them *mudzimu*, the spirits. She don't look like anything that work in hair salon. When she talk, she speak slow, you can't hurry she; she can even wave death away like it is some nuisance fly. But Tsitsi say that she is the fastest weaver in the salon. She carry the spirit world with she and wear this old funny air that force you to pay attention to every word that she say

44

because it come out and drop like stone falling on concrete floor.

'*Mamuka seyi?*' Aleck greet she at the door.

She shuffle into the house in flowing layers of clothes and red dustcoat as Aleck lead she into the kitchen with his hands clasped together in respectful way. Tsitsi follow and the kitchen door is closed.

Shingi say MaiMusindo is old-school kind of Zimbabwean who think she hold all the wisdom and want to help everyone. She want to help Tsitsi since the day they meet at Brixton market. That was the day when MaiMusindo is buying vegetables at crowded stall and Tsitsi is also looking for tomatoes. When MaiMusindo's mobile go off and she let rip in old and deep Shona, Tsitsi nearly jump on the old woman with big rural happiness. That's what homesickness do. Tsitsi – she don't know how to keep things inside – she roll out she whole story and MaiMusindo now think she can help. MaiMusindo want Aleck to help Tsitsi go back to she aunt but Aleck is busy all the time and have no time, that's how Farayi see it. But MaiMusindo don't understand that she is sticking she nose in people's business; Tsitsi's aunt is not going to like this style, me I know.

Aleck come out of the kitchen talk looking like he regret that he take this Tsitsi thing under his wing. His neck is deep inside his shoulder with stress.

Even if it was me who have take Tsitsi into house because of sympathy me I will not want to take she back to family that have mess up she life like this. She is damaged goods and things like this can cause lot of vex and leave heaps of trousers ruined from all the pacing about and shouting between family members. Even worse, Tsitsi's aunt is going to accuse Aleck of trying to ruin she marriage by pushing Tsitsi back into she house.

MaiMusindo walk out of the kitchen and throw in this mother kind of greeting into our room.

'*Makadii ko vana vangu?*'

'*Tiripo makadii,*' Shingi and Farayi answer like choirboys.

'*Takasimba?*'

Farayi jump up and lug his firewood bum out of our room to go and greet she properly. Shingi also feel oblige to follow and go to stand by our door. Me I hang back because I don't know this funny woman.

Farayi and Shingi make the usual respectful greetings that you do with elderly person and shake hands. She look absent-minded, or tired. But she is old spirit; she presence make everyone stand still and quiet and wait for she to talk.

Now I creep in behind Shingi to see.

I'm still hiding behind Shingi and suddenly I can't tell if MaiMusindo is staring at me or at Shingi. She tongue come out: 'I have hear about you from Tsitsi. Your people – where they hail from?'

She is talking to Shingi.

'Chi . . . Chipinge,' Shingi say with big football-size eyes.

MaiMusindo nod slow. Then she wander out of conversation in funny absent-minded way and everyone don't know if she's talking to us or to sheself, or if she is just rethinking what she have just said. Then suddenly she awaken from she trance and she sneeze in funny way. She remember the point that she is wanting to make now: 'Tsitsi has tell me about you,' she say to Shingi as she turn round and head for the door, leaving everyone under spell.

'What did you say?' Shingi ask Tsitsi.

'Nothing. I don't know.' She shrug she shoulders and hop around on one leg like naughty likkle flea and stomp upstairs to she room.

'It's because of Shingi's Chipinge roots,' Aleck say.

Farayi start making fun of Shingi and saying that maybe

46

MaiMusindo want to learn tricks from Shingi because people with Chipinge roots is supposed to have dangerous knowledge of sorcery and stuff, especially *mamhepo*, the avenging spirits.

Farayi laugh all morning. Aleck now also jump into making fun of Shingi saying he have *mamhepo* spirit pursuing him; Farayi is making joke but anyone can sniff sniff that Aleck really mean it. Shingi don't find it funny.

Mamhepo; the winds – someone can raise them against you and your family if you kill they innocent relative. That's what Aleck say as he pace about in our room with hands in his pockets.

Farayi keep quiet now. Aleck continue his lecture in his style of talking without looking at person that he talk to.

There is grandmaster Banda who can do all that stuff and heaps more, me I know. He live in the dry and dusty malaria district of Chipinge, the rural home of Shingi's family. He is witchcraft grandmaster with big reputation. He can shrink any beast down to the size of grain of sand. He do that to dozens of herd of cattle, and use his wife's straw broom to sweep them into old envelope and then board bus to whatever part of the country he choose. On arriving he undo the spell and sell them cattle having suffer zero transport costs. Many people go to Banda but some of them things they ask him to do don't involve shrink cow, but the frightful business of invoke *mamhepo* for families that want revenge if family member has been killed by someone. They say some fat cat try to patent Banda's cow-shrinking magic but get stuck when, while filling them patent forms, he feel desperate to pee and run to toilet only to discover that his tool has vanish clean off him. Me I know all this but I don't go *paparapapara* showing off like Aleck.

Banda is big man. But sometimes his magic don't work as expected. Especially with them other things that is not the winds. Like when he shrink cattle down to the size of grain of sand and sweep them into envelope. In some cases, even if the cattle reduce in size, they weight remain the same, so people find that the bus they board, under weight of tons of cow, either break down or is not able to crawl out of the bus terminus.

6

Me I get £2.45 per hour. Eight hours per day. Five days per week. That make £98 per week. But after they do emergency tax code it come to about £68.

You spend them weeks shifting mud with shovels and sweat beads come out of every pore in the body because you is putting out heaps of effort while your buttocks point to high heaven and migrant flesh start to stink around you as shirts and underpants get damp. Here you quickly know that the weight of your buttocks increase by the hour and come down only by night when you is sandwiched between blanket and mattress.

Then one day you hear: Take them your things and move it. That's what they say to us in Wimbledon. The graft end without warning. Everyone on the site have to move it now after we go to work one morning to find the site closed. One servant come out of the house, and looking pleased, tell us that there is disagreement between the owner of house and our employer because them pavings that we have lay and the retaining walls that we have build is not up to standard. And most of them plants that we have plant in the past months have dead, he add. He have been tell to advise us to contact our employer, in Romford, if we have any issue to complain about.

We have been stitch up, I know straight away. But there is nothing we can do, so we scatter without quarrel.

Samuel, who is from Senegal, tell us that there is another company in Finsbury Park that is looking for labourers. There is also one street corner in Mile End where if you is foreign labourer you can go and hang around with your toolbox. Soon some van come and someone, sitting in the van, will point at people that look like they is up to hard graft. If you is lucky you get picked. We don't have no toolboxes to pose with on this street, so we don't go there. Also there is now too many Polish builders to compete with there, someone say. And they all have toolboxes.

Finsbury Park is better, that's what everyone agree as we wait for bus. But with this kind of graft, now I see there is big danger that you can work until you grow horns and still you won't catch US$5,000. But Shingi is keen on Finsbury Park so me I keep quiet.

If you find graft as porter at some hotels that is visit by Saudi princes then you can land your native bum in butter because them princes give good tips and can drop £1,000 in your pocket if you is sweet when you carry they luggage for them. That's what I have hear. But right now I don't even know which hotel to look out for.

The bus arrive and we queue up to get in. Suleiman is first. He flash his fake bus pass and immediately put this hard-set look on his face, looking straight ahead rigid as he march like soldier past the bus driver.

'Excuse me, sir, can I see your pass?' The driver stop him. It's at moments like this that the city can get chance to break your disguise with them questions: what's your name, sir; where did you get this, sir; you know this is crime offence, sir?

'Where did you get your card from, sir?' the driver say playing big mischief with politeness. This title that the mud-shifting boy have been given is too heavy for him now.

'Sir?' The driver pull down his glasses in professor-style so they sit low on his nose.

This 'sir' thing put Suleiman in proper straitjacket. His tongue

50

weigh same as hippo and he can't lift it now. He turn his head to the door, spot an opening and go for it. His trousers explode and rip at the crotch as he leap over pram. He land on pavement, stumble and regain his balance. Quality people in nice clothes at the front of the queue have already turn into heap of arms and legs on the pavement. They struggle to free theyselfs from each each as mud-shifting boy take off. Frightened, he plunge into them pedestrians, shoots past pub, past the supermarket, he take a corner and take his ruined trousers elsewhere. Near me the mother of the baby in the pram is like ice sculpture; she is so pale she is nearly transparent. Not one drop of blood in she face.

One by one we fall out of queue and march to another bus stop.

Harare North is big con. We have already put many Mars bars inside people's pockets, and now look.

We show up at contractor's plant yard in Finsbury Park, along with handful of them other guys from the Wimbledon graft. Some foreman with fierce face say he is looking for people who want to work on drain repair project; workers who is prepared for challenging work; excavating and stripping them old drainpipes out of the earth, laying new ones, and going down pipes to remove blockage when necessary. All for £2.40 per hour, take it or leave it. I have not been in London long time but me I can smell big con from miles. Especially that we was getting £2.45 per hour in Wimbledon. And that was the lowest rate Shingi have ever do.

'Does anyone have any question?' the foreman ask, with cigarette in mouth. He don't sound English. The cigarette in his mouth is in big trouble – on one end he have put it on fire and on the other he is chewing it with them long brown teeth. Me I am not doing no graft for this man, I make up my mind quick.

'Does anyone have any question?' Them migrants fidget and

grind they teeth; the foreman have hit they heads and get them out of gear and they is not able to say anything.

The foreman nod with big satisfaction and give the cigarette another crazy bite while he scan them faces and smile. He bite and chew. He bite again. The migrants shake and blink like convicts.

'Hands up people with work permits?' the foreman demand.

Shingi have one finger raised in the air.

'OK, only three. Rest of you have to get new IDs. Passports. We do it for you but it cost you £300.'

Me I am not having none of that con, I tell Shingi when we leave. I warn him to stay away from people with them funny habits like biting cigarettes. That is suspect style. But Shingi say he have do lots of graft in London before. How many graft have you done in London? he ask me.

I can't argue against that. Shingi can be stubborn; just like them millipedes. Mother spend decades sweeping millipedes off she doorstep. You sweep millipede away and half-hour later it come back to your doorstep, right where it was. Grandmother keep telling Mother that if you don't want millipede to come back you also have to throw away the straw broom that you use to sweep it away. 'But here in the township how many straw brooms will I have to buy to throw away with every *zongororo*?' Mother always ask, shaking she head. Sometimes she throw the broom away to make Grandmother happy but the *zongororo* always come back to the same spot, until someone step on it.

Now, me I also throw away my straw broom and watch.

Civilian people sometimes don't have nothing to say about bold plans. I lay my big plan to Shingi and ask what he think: I have to start checking out which hotels to mau-mau. But Shingi don't have nothing to say.

Every day now, Shingi come back from his new graft and tell

everyone about how good them fake EU passports is because one of his workmates have even used it to go to Belgium and come back and no one catch him. He have heaps to say about this.

Big ginger for this idea of having fake EU passport start to grow inside Shingi's head. He don't even need the fake passport except maybe to catch illiterate girls by telling them jazz numbers saying that he is French man.

At first I ignore this talk because such stories is all over Harare North. Soon the idea start to grow into proper tree and it bust out of the back of his head, tilting his head back. Now he can't pull his head back to look down where he is stepping. But because he look after me, buying all the food and paying the rent, I don't want to upset him and say this is getting out of order. So me I sweet him and tell him that maybe soon he will have French passport too and become big Frenchman. He go kak kak kak about this. Soon I call him Mr Chirac; you know what it's like when you have to keep big cheer on the face of your comrade while you is planning next move.

Maybe when I get French passport I give you my Zimbabwe passport so you can use it to look for job, Shingi laugh. He have hear from his graft that everyone that don't have the right papers have got French passports organised for them now. French passport is easy to thief, that's what people that sell fake passports on Tottenham Court Road say.

Maybe when you get back home you can tell big story about life in Harare North; big story about how you can become labourer, sewage drain cleaner and then French President; being many people in one person.

I tell Mr Chirac this because these kind of stories rolled into one can be sweet story if telled while one big mug of *chibuku* brew is passing around the table until the teller have also forget which part of story is just sweet jazz number and which is true; when you only tell truth by accident.

Now give me pocket money for small packet of cigarettes, I ask Shingi after giving him this suggestion.

Before I have even finish doing list of hotels, Shingi disappear, and in the house President Chirac take his place. It is up to me to feel free to use Shingi's Zimbabwean passport and National Insurance number whenever I feel like I want to.

'I . . . I am not original n-native now,' Chirac tell us all, Tsitsi, Aleck, Farayi and me. 'W . . . we is not the same any more, Aleck. Wh . . . while yo . . . you graft hard in Harare North, me I will soon be hitting French wine and wiping my bottom with them butter croissants,' Chirac say, leaping into squiggly dance and disappearing to the kitchen.

7

History is littered with them ruined underpants of small people leaping about in vex style and trying to save they bread from the long throats of big people. Me I have already lose one pair of them underpants trying to save my Mars bars from long throats. That is one pair of underpants too many. Now is time for new tactics. I am about to finish investigating which hotels to check out.

Shingi have give me £20 to go buy food for us for the week but that is too much money so me I only use £15 and make saving of £5. When I come from Tesco supermarket I can see our house, this Shingi's head, looking at me like it accuse me of things.

I step inside, put bread on table and drag myself onto the cupboard by the kitchen sink and sit with my back to the window. Everyone else have go to they graft and Tsitsi is washing them dishes in the kitchen. Sometimes when she wash dishes she also start talking to me about how she used to climb them guava trees when she was small.

'Just like boys,' she say.

'You wanted to be boy?'

'No; boys always get cysts on they eyes.'

'Why?'

'Because they always peep up skirt of girl if she climb tree.'

Me I have nothing to say. She mind is already made up on everything: boys get cysts on they eyes; if you is small girl and take chicken egg that has just been laid and rub onto your chest you never grow breasts; if you is boy and rub the egg on your chin you never grow beard. Evil spirits can imitate voices of people that you know and call your name at night and if you answer your voice will never come back. Owls can call your name too. If someone jump over you while you is sitting down you will never grow taller unless they undo they jump.

Tsitsi start singing as she wash them dishes. She always sing them songs that she have carry from she rural hills where them women sing while carrying they buckets of water from borehole. But some days she sing them real ignorant songs by villagers that have never even peep inside classroom window:

> Look the train go *geje geje* rolling through dusty land
> Look the white man's iron puff smoke
> Look it grind itself through the hills
> Look the puffing iron take my child away to the city.

Now this big moth fly through the air and land on she shoulders. I stretch my hand so I can pick it off but Tsitsi brush me away with wet hand.

I take it off myself, she say without even looking at me. Then she continue washing up and singing.

Tsitsi finish washing and go out to visit MaiMusindo and she friends at the hair salon. I have nothing to do; I spend the afternoon in our room lying down and reading one of them Yellow Pages books that junk mail people sometimes leave outside our door. There is hotels inside it.

Shingi's passport and National Insurance card is on my pillow while I read hard and make final list of hotels.

Tsitsi come back inside the house. She have come with bunch of sunflowers. She throw the bunch of them flowers on Farayi's bed and also throw she baby there. I rub my eyes because I was about to fall asleep. Now I feel like I want to be useful so instead of just talk talk talk with she, me I open my suitcase, get my shirt out and start to sew back my button that have fall off. I light my cigarette; now smoke is coming out of my nose and mouth.

Where you get all them flowers?

From the salon. Eunice go to buy flowers this morning to decorate salon but flower vendor is friend so he give away too many, she say.

MaiMusindo give them to me because no one else in salon want them.

MaiMusindo have also give Tsitsi bottle of some funny perfume – *Moschino Parfum* it say on the label. It look like old people's kind of perfume but me I don't say nothing.

She go to kitchen and come back with knife so she can start cut stem ends of them sunflowers. But before Tsitsi have even sit down, the baby start to cry. She sit on Farayi's bed and start to feed him.

What's his name?

Tafadzwa.

She start singing to she baby:

Dance around together
Holding hands together
Dance around together
Holding hands together
Tissue, tissue, we all fall down.

I know that from when I was smaller than teaspoon, I tell she.

Yeeessss! she eyes bulge and she start talking with hand and all: yari yari yari we hold hands together in circle and go round and round singing *Dance around together*; oh when it get to *tissue* you get ready because when *we all fall down* comes you all crouch down; oh then you go on and on again.

No, you throw yourself complete down to ground.

But your clothes get dirty, she say in very sharp way.

Tsitsi start talking that baby language to she baby. Me I am smoking and sewing. When she finish feeding baby she sit him on the bed with Farayi's pillow behind because the baby always fall backwards.

My screwdriver is on the floor. Tsitsi pick it and give to she baby to play with because it have bright yellow-and-black handle and babies like them such things like that. Now the baby is trying to pick it up but only manage to dribble all over it and me I don't like baby dribble on my screwdriver. But I don't say nothing.

Tsitsi start cutting them flowers and putting them inside big jug.

You hungry? she ask me when she have finish cutting them flowers.

Me I don't want to break them these house rules or else people start throwing ugly kind of mouth around, I tell she.

Tsitsi curl and twiddle she small toes and say nothing. There is funny silence between us. Me I don't want to talk too much to Tsitsi about them house rules because I have to be careful with she; she is bubbly bubbly likkle mother but she is also just simple girl that can ruin your life by telling people things without knowing that she is ruining you. You know that kind of madness that is always inside them rural people. I don't want no one to start saying that I only stay inside the house so I can hit they food while they is doing graft. Me I am principled man.

Tsitsi come back from the kitchen eating bread and baked beans. She start to talk about the rat that have been eating food in the kitchen, how it get she head out of gear, the rat manage to do it even if she put the food on the highest shelf in the kitchen; the following day she find it have been nibbled.

I don't have answers for these questions so I give she them

58

one-word answers and small grunts and try to sew while she go yep yep yep yep. She is now sitting in funny cross-legged way on bed, with she pointy breasts jumping out at me and she have no idea that this kind of sitting can give people funny ideas. But it don't do nothing to me because me I am not civilian person but military person. Tsitsi, she is just rural mother. She is also just one small child. I don't need to worry about Tsitsi. Me I am not civilian.

Chirac is civilian person and have this tree growing out of his head making him not able to see where he is putting his foot. Fix him up with this rural thing maybe he can also drop me cigarette pocket money. It don't matter that he still have not buy the French passport. But Shingi is scared of Aleck because he is still not good at defending himself if someone start to accuse him of leading the child, Tsitsi, astray. Even at school, after Thoko beat him up, Shingi still don't know how to fight for himself. Even when I'm trying to teach him every week at school. His stepbrother Chamu, who is one year ahead of us, also try to teach him how to fight because Chamu is not always there to protect him, but that never work. Only one time in his life Shingi have stand up for himself and that was the last time. That was few years after we leave school for ever. Shingi have got graft as tea boy at Central African Pharmaceutical Society (CAPS) and for some funny reason he spill tea on company's biggest boss and his big visitor; the whole teapot splash all over the big man's desk and trousers. His visitor's trousers too. And important papers. Everything get wet and this is big mess-up and of course if you do big mess-up you get fired. One week after he have been fired them people at the local beer hall start throwing that usual mouth about: oh poor Shingi; the winds that he get from his father now giving him bad luck; yeee he will never have steady life; yeee maybe he don't get fired because of tea but because of all that liquid paraffin he thief. People was saying that because Shingi had also start to sell liquid paraffin that he bring from CAPS. No one know how he get it, but he get it and people like to use it on they skin.

Then when Shingi come to the beer hall after losing graft someone make big mistake of making fun of him by saying now that he have no more liquid paraffin, maybe his family going to start using cooking oil on they skin. Because he don't do talk, Shingi jump into this style of big quiet vex. Now everyone start going kak kak kak and Shingi don't know how to deal with this and soon pull out of his pocket the oldest style in the book; you know how someone get upset by someone but they don't know how to deal with it except to play out they is now possessed by old family spirit. Shingi groan, spit and growl until them veins in his neck writhe under the skin like fat worms, and the guy that make fun of Shingi is still laughing because he think this is big pretence. But before he know it Shingi have pick up half brick and hit him square on his face.

Shingi spend six months in prison for that but when he come out he have change style of talking and now don't say even one word more than is necessary if he is talking to you; no one want to throw they mouth around in front of him now because they know he can waste your face if you hassle him.

But this is Harare North and people change back into they old self here.

I finish sewing my button on and decide to do them others that look like they is wanting to fall too. Then Tsitsi go to kitchen again to make milk for baby. She shout from the kitchen asking again if me I am hungry.

What you going to say if Aleck find out you been giving me food? I shout back. She don't answer. This is food that Aleck have buy, but that's not the problem. Tsitsi have also been worryful that they is not going to have enough food this week because Aleck have send heap of money back home to pay for some stand in Highfield township. £1,000, that's what he wire back for the stand. US$1,910. But it hit his pocket hard because now every food item that he and Tsitsi buy have already get affected except the old bread and beans which everyone is tired of. Meat is already out of the shopping list that week and Tsitsi worryful she is becoming big burden on Aleck now. But maybe Aleck don't worry too much because now Tsitsi have start to bring in small money by going out to the salon; MaiMusindo and them other women is helping she rent out the baby to other women that want to apply for council flats as single mothers. For £50, any woman can take Tsitsi's baby to the Lambeth Housing Department and play out to be single mother, fill them forms and take baby back to salon as soon as she have been interview.

I finish sewing the buttons and I am putting my needle and thread back inside my suitcase and Tsitsi is again sitting in crazy rural way – crouching in front of me in she lopsided skirt that is full of lint, bobbles and all the fluff. She is feeding milk to she baby.

You can sometimes go through life and never get laid. That's Shingi. He never get over the fear of girls that Thoko put inside him since we was at school and end up only trying to make people laugh. I know of people who have pay up heaps of money to lose they virginity. Like the blind singer in Harare that end up paying US$200 for people to organise him woman.

But I have not even have chance to talk to Shingi and things happen fast. The cigarette-biting people – they exorcise Chirac out of the native without no warning. Just like that.

During graft, Shingi and his friends have always been digging out heaps of them drainpipes, repair some, lay new ones and getting used to crawling in them dark holes to clear them blocked drains. Always with long rope tied to foot in case you get overcome down there and pass out in the slurry, mud and poo. Now they get frogmarched out of the site by hard men holding scaffold poles. They have been forced back into they original native selfs again. And it's all because they have been talk talk talk too much about them French passports until someone hear of it and sell them out. Cigarette-biting people don't trust none of them now because they think one of them tip them immigration people. President Chirac vanish. Now the original native appear again.

Because this is Shingi, and you know what Shingi is like, it take him days to come out and tell what happen. After all them squiggly dances and talk of hitting French food he feel embarrassed now to tell us that he have lose his graft. Me I knew this was going to happen. But me I don't want to talk; I throw away my straw broom long time ago and leave the *zongororo* to do what it want.

On this day when Tsitsi have spend all afternoon sitting in front of me in that crazy way, that's when Shingi's story come out. I am still talking to she thinking that Shingi have go to graft but he only have go for graft hunt without telling no one. He have been doing this style for days, now it come out. Now he arrive pushing this face that is as long as shield of Matabele warrior.

Where have you abandon your spear and knobkerrie and do you know that this is one offence that is punished by death if you had live during time of *Mfecane*? That's the first question you want to ask when you see someone carrying that face. But Shingi don't look like he is in mood for jokes so I say nothing.

We have not even start starving but his face already look thin and his lips dry and cracked; now his teethies suddenly is crowded inside his mouth. He have come straight inside house, remove his dirty boots and disappear inside the bathroom to have shower. Tsitsi take she baby upstairs and leave us alone.

All that time I don't know what this Shingi thing is all about but can sniff sniff that this have something to do with his graft.

Now I have to do something to make Shingi feel better. I open my suitcase, take out my screwdriver, grab some old newspaper and Shingi's boots, and I start to scrap the mud off. I do this for ages but Shingi don't come out to see. Then me I get tired, put the screwdriver back inside my suitcase, wrap up the dirt and throw it in the bin outside.

Now I hear him coming. Me I jump off my suitcase and go to the kitchen to make him coffee. When I walk back, he is sitting still. I hold out the cup of coffee to him and he ask me to put it down on the floor next to his feeties. I have forget to buy milk, so the coffee that I make him has black and shiny metallic surface like used engine oil. I sit down on my suitcase and watch him. He have trace of sneer on corner of his nose.

He never touch the coffee but only thumb his nose once and lie down on the bed.

Shingi only start to talk the following day. Now he tell how cigarette-biting foreman march them out because someone sell them out to immigration people and there is going to be some raid soon. One of the foreman's people have dog and when Shingi try to explain that he have proper papers the man don't listen and nearly let they dog loose on him. Shingi is in big trauma; even today when I ask him what kind of dog this was, he only say it have very big mouth. This kind of end have been easy to see for everyone but Shingi.

In the evening when Farayi and Aleck come from graft, Farayi sympathise big time with Shingi. But head boy Aleck not very impressed about all this. He is worried for his rent money.

8

'BBC graft for £8 per hour. Immediate start, and it's in Croydon.' That's what Aleck tell us. He is trying hard to head us in BBC direction and Shingi is drooling now.

'The fly that land on dollop of poo is the lucky one,' I tell Aleck. 'The one that land on honey is in big trouble. That's the tricky thing about living in Harare North. But some of us, we have to ask the question: you want to do something – what is better, to try doing it your own way and risk finding small success, or to do it in undignified pooful way and find big success?'

Both Shingi and Aleck get the score quick and stop all this BBC talk. Me I am principled man.

The Savoy Hotel, the Ritz Hotel, myhotel Chelsea, Crowne Plaza Shoreditch and Westbury Hotel. That's the list of hotels that I plan to mau-mau. But Shingi don't have ginger for talking this. Me I think maybe it's time to cook supper for him.

In the fridge there is still some of the beefsteak that Shingi have buy on his way from work some few days before. Like usual, I take my screwdriver out of my suitcase to use it to make steak tender before cooking. I pound the meat with the screwdriver's heavy handle and after that I stab stab stab the steak with the other end of the screwdriver.

Then I fry it nice. I also make vegetable relish and when I lick the wooden spoon me I know this is number-one stuff. While all this is getting ready I decide to cook bit of rice but I cannot use our pot because it get burnt in the morning and so have dark layer of porridge at the bottom. The worst thing you can do is use burnt porridge pot because whatever you cook inside it start to smell of black porridge and no one want to eat it. Instead of rice, I cut some bread for us and take it to our room where we eat silent.

We have not yet find mattress in them rubbish skips for me, so I lie beside Shingi in bed because he share his bed with me.

I try to light up the mood by making joke about how if the cigarette-biting man run rings around Chirac's head like that, maybe Chirac was fake Frenchman. Big mistake. Shingi blow his top off and tell me to start bringing in money for food and rent instead of sit on my tail all day and only waiting to crack jokes, play food games with him and pretending I possess him.

Now we stop all them jokes and food games. Even when I know I still possess him.

Food is tricky subject; things get funny over it. Even before Shingi lose his graft, food sometimes make conversation funny. And that's not only with me but also Aleck, Tsitsi and Farayi. But that's not big surprise to me. Or even Shingi. The two of us have had chance of witnessing them troubles that food can cause from long time.

One morning I get shocked to find that Shingi's bearded mother, MaiShingi, is involved in fight with she new husband over bread. MaiShingi's husband is about to go to his graft as commuter bus conductor, and she is getting ready for she day. She do people's hair from home and one customer have already arrive wanting to have she hair straightened.

I am waiting for Shingi and his stepbrother Chamu to finish eating they porridge so we can go to school together when Shingi's stepfather, in his blue uniform, order his wife to cut him two slices of bread while he get dressed. He dash through the lounge as he say this.

'What?' MaiShingi clap she hands in big surprise to show this is bad bad omen. 'Me slicing bread for you?' she bawl. She can be proper fishwife sometimes.

Now, she husband is stunned and don't know what style he have been hit with. He is not sure what to do in the front of MaiShingi's customer who is sitting in the lounge, pretending to peel off nail polish from she fingernails because she is stewing up in unease. And the lounge, which is also hair salon and always filled with smells of burnt hair and chemicals, now also have the new smell of food quarrel.

'Aah, MaiShingi?' he try to warn she, but MaiShingi don't bother answering; she pick she new shaver from the table and disappear into the bathroom. Now anyone can sniff sniff that MaiShingi's husband is going to be worryful all day if peace is ever possible inside house that have two people who shave beard every morning. That's the kind of thing food quarrel can do and complicate everything. People always fight over food; if it is scarce they fight over them crumbs, and if there's enough of it, people fight over who get to put it on the plate and for who. And if there's just too much of it, people bawl horror and want to fight them supermarkets for trying to fatten them.

The problem is that disagreement over food always end up with innocent people hurt. Food arguments don't fail to have victim. Shingi's stepfather, after the fight with wife, he run off to work with big vex on his face. That day, all them fare dodgers and poor mothers that rely on begging for conductors' kindness to have free ride with they children is in for big shock, me I know straight away.

That's food. So when food talk make Shingi sore like that, I step with care.

*　　*　　*

Me I wake up, I get up, I get clothed, I tie my shoelaces and step off out of the house. You can't mau-mau like hungry man when you have got full stomach, so I don't eat nothing that morning.

Money is like termite. The more desire you have to catch it, the more you scare it down into its hole. You don't try to catch it by its head, but let it crawl out of the hole first. That's what I'm reasoning as I walk down Brixton Road. You have to have big patient style with these things.

Then there is this news–animal that follow your every step from Zimbabwe, hiding in the dark tailwinds behind you. You can't see it but only hear its footsteps; you stop, the footsteps stop, you walk and you hear them footsteps again. All the news of emeralds or diamonds and the government wanting to take Mother's village – is this propaganda or what? You have to catch the termite before this thing come out for you, that's the catch. Otherwise it scatter your mind all over like leafs at the mercy of the winds and you lose what you believe in and have no weapon to fight with. Then you never get out of Harare North.

Today I have to find hotel to mau-mau. When I leave the house Shingi is still in funny mood and say he have headache. I offer him cigarette but he just shake his head tight. He is making big play out of studying ceiling, clearing his throat and swallowing all the time like he want to say something but he never do. Me I leave him alone.

Farayi and Aleck have already go to graft and Tsitsi have again go to rent she baby at the hair salon.

As I'm stepping off down them pavements and reasoning me I don't know that by the time I come back in the evening I will find that there's also now some Judas inside our house. Someone have been going through my suitcase I can tell straight away; they have leave my screwdriver pointing to the opposite way from how I leave it. I forget to lock it before I leave. Someone have sniff sniff and look inside my suitcase and they even thief my US$9.55. You can take the money but don't look inside my suitcase.

Me I am not civilian person; so I don't go *paparapapara* panicking. The past always give you the tools to handle the present. Add small bit of crooked touch to what you do and everyone soon get startled into silence and start paying proper attention and respect to you. Every jackal boy know that style; drop in crazy laughter in some crazy place during interrogation and any traitor will listen up. It's not accident that 'skill' and 'slaughter' start with a crooked letter. Every jackal boy know that too. Remove the crooked touch from each of them those two words and suddenly you kill laughter.

When I come back from mau-mauing hotels, Shingi start drinking that old brandy he buy last month. Aleck is in the shower and Tsitsi and Farayi is cooking in the kitchen.

I don't want to talk to no one about my day. I have spend all day looking for hotel and can't find nothing because they is hidden. I only hit one hotel after I see one man that look like he's from Saudi Arabia going inside. I step inside the hotel and I know straight away that this is visited only by quality people that only poo pure strawberries and fresh cream. There is one beautiful woman being helped at the reception. Me I'm still looking at this beautiful thing and suddenly I don't know what happen next because before I even know it two fat bouncers in uniform have throw me out onto the street. It happen so fast, I am stunned. Maybe they even hit me on the head with some frying pan or something because my head still feel dizzy now. But now look what I find inside our house?

Everyone say they never touch my suitcase and Shingi say he don't see nothing all afternoon. Because the person that look inside my suitcase did not search the bottom, me I don't want to push it.

Before we go to bed Shingi is drunk now in pathetic way. He get up from the bed and go to kitchen and stagger about in very careless way. Then he make mistake of dragging his foot on board that is loose and some funny noise come out of his mouth. He limp back and collapse down on mattress. It's one big splinter, one centimetre or more into his foot.

The best thing to remove it is maybe the needle and that's what Shingi ask for.

'My needle is lost inside my suitcase, me I can't find it,' I tell him. I go to the kitchen and take two knives. One belong to Aleck and Tsitsi and is one of them things with clip-point blade. The other, ours, is normal big bread knife.

I walk back into our room whetting them two knives together and Shingi recoil in drunk horror.

Easy, boss, everything is under control, me I say and go kak kak kak. I have do this before – I make one clean cut along it splinter with this knife then I spade it out with this.

Shingi have heap of suspicion on his face.

Me I have no time to waste with drunk person. If you don't trust my skill then just say so, I tell him.

I try to cut sharp line along the firewood, and try do it at some angle so that I end up cutting towards it once I get under skin.

Shingi's skin under his foot is dry and cracked and hard like tortoise shell. So no matter how careful I am, I just can't get past it. I tell him that I now have to put more force because it look like he have tortoise ancestor somewhere in the past. I sit on his leg so that I hold it tight in case he try jump about.

Now I have his leg tight like vice grip.

Now admit that you are the one that look inside my suitcase

70

or I push this splinter ten miles inside your foot, me I go kak kak kak into the ceiling.

Shingi try to jump about but this is vice grip.

OK OK it's me it's me, he surrender quick.

Me I was only joking, you coward. But I still remove the splinter for you.

Things start to go wrong because Shingi can't keep his foot still as I cut into his foot. He thrash about really bad and I am struggling to hold his leg tight with my legs. Then blood start to go everywhere and me I have to stop because I don't want to touch no blood. Shingi have been in prison, and everyone that go to prison always come out with Aids, me I know. I have to let Shingi pull the splinter out with his own fingers.

Aids also end with crooked letter. That can add bit of the crooked touch to your style if you know that tomorrow you will be gone. Those traitors know that too.

9

'Do you really know him?' I ask Shingi but he is just twitching his tail like proud thing and ignore me. I don't say nothing too. He think he know everything about this granite-jawed bitter old Zimbabwean man that work part-time with Aleck. That's the Zimbabwean that now live in Brixton after running away from police back home. He is the one that hook up Shingi and Aleck together and live at Tulse Hill Estate and have very impatient style. One blazing eye and greying stubble; he remind you of many things.

He also do the asylum style – that's how he get the council flat that he live in because Lambeth Council getting a fair share of Zimbabwean asylum seekers these days. But he have fall out of love with Zimbabwe, don't want to know it no more and don't even want to be known. Last time we visit him our conversation end in funny silence. That's because he is that kind of person that you can buy beer for and say I know you but they will throw back at you some rough mouth like 'You say you know me, has your mother ever cook *sadza* for me?' He is so rough you can't admit that he don't want to be your friend and you still buy him four more beers hoping that maybe you have make friendship. Still he don't want to know you.

I know him from home this old man. His flat, that's where Shingi say he is going to spend the day because he is in funny mood since I help him remove that splinter. He is limping about and his eye accuse me of damaging his foot.

Before Shingi have limp off to the old man, me I step out of the house and off to Paul and Sekai.

Now I have to make new plan and make peace with Paul and Sekai; you can never trust people that is not your relative in foreign places. Especially with all them these small betrayals going on inside our house. Shingi is worryful, you can see. All them big promises that he have make to his family that he will send them money, they is hanging around his neck, and he don't want news getting back home that he have lose his graft again because that have already happen three times now since he come to London. But I don't get the score why he behave like this to me.

Sekai is on the phone and old Paul is at the computer, poking keyboard with two fingers like policeman. Paul have disappointed look on his face when he let me in at the door and walk back to the computer saying he just want to finish off something quickly. That's when Sekai leave the phone and jump on me, cross-examining me on why I just leave them without no warning and if I was wanting to burn they house down because I leave petrol behind; what kind of thing is that? Now, you don't let no one talk to you like so if you is not depending on they food no more.

'Don't rush to swallow things before you have even chew them proper because you will choke and get us very worryful,' I tell she straight and square. 'The petrol was inside house because me I forget to take it with me; Aleck was coming to pick me in his car but run out of petrol by Stratford station. I was going to bring him the petrol but then he phone saying he have manage to top up.' I spin she head dizzy now.

She nearly choke on that but suddenly now she have big ginger to point out them things that is not adding up in my story, trying to catch me out, spinning some jazz number and make me feel cheap. But me I'm doing them swanky ninja moves inside my head; ducking, diving and doing cartwheels so she end up clutching thin air. Then she start taking me to task for bad manners because I only tell them by email that I have leave them.

Paul come to my rescue because now he can see that this has become embarrassing because his wife will try to throttle me if he don't stop she.

Sekai get ready for night shift and she leave without saying goodbye to me.

'There is mail for you in the kitchen,' Paul tell soon after Sekai have bang the door on the way out. It's one letter from my uncle. When I leave home, he had promise that he will help organise *umbuyiso* ceremony for Mother. Now he say he is not sure if it's useful for him to start organising anything because people in the village where Mother is buried have already been telled that they have to prepare to be resettled any time.

'This village, Mother's family have been there since 1947 when they was moved from fertile land in Mazoe because the land have been given as reward to some British Second World War veteran. Now they have to move again?'

Paul nothing to say to me about this.

'Soon Mother's grave maybe end up being dig up by some machine, get wash away by rain and she bones come out in the open and get bleached by sun just like bones of dead bird and no one is going to care.'

When I tell Paul about what happen when I try to find hotel where Saudi princes give fat tips, he nearly fall off his chair laughing. Now I have to stop talking about this because people think that I am dunderhead. But when I leave me and Paul is still talking in civilised way.

I say sorry for how I leave them last time.

'You know anything about Uncle Nhamo?' That's what Paul ask as he walk me to Tube station. I don't know where this question come from or if this is trick question or what. Uncle Nhamo kill himself when I am still the size of teaspoon. Everything that I have hear about him is funny because everyone going hush hush. People say he have the winds.

'Yes I know about Uncle Nhamo.' I don't want Paul to start accuse me of not knowing family members like them young people do these days. He's old-fashioned in that kind of thing even though he is not old.

He kick some stone on the pavement in that way like, OK, let's leave that one alone. It's funny behaviour by Paul. And me I don't want to talk about this Uncle Nhamo dead guy.

'What will happen to all them family graves in Mother's village and why is Uncle doing nothing?'

But Paul say nothing. Even Uncle Nhamo is buried in Mother's village.

When the past always tower over you like a mother of children of darkness, all you can do is hide under she skirt. There you see them years hanging in great big folds of skin and when you pop your head out of under the skirt you don't tell no one what you have see because that is where you come from. You tell them and people will treat you funny. Especially civilian people. You don't tell no one about the past or you frighten them. Me I don't say even one word about the past to anyone inside our house. Things is still funny in here. Shingi have just send chunk of his savings to family back home. The Western Union form is there on our bed.

I have buy sausages, do you want?

Shingi just lie in bed quiet and don't say nothing to me but only shake his head with funny grin on his face; one of them grins that stay on the face even if the owner of the face have stop smiling two months ago. Maybe it's because there is still no lead to follow regarding graft.

We need to clean our house. We have to sweep the floors because they is full of dirt and it's hard to think straight inside this house, Shingi say now. You need to clean the inside of your head, I don't say.

It's morning, everyone have go to graft, Tsitsi have go to hang out at hair salon and it's only me and Shingi in this house and I'm still reasoning what kind of plan to make now.

Shingi expect me to go get the broom and start the cleaning. Time stop suddenly. Outside, the city rattle on as usual: doors slamming on faces of people that is mau-mauing for graft, rail tracks red hot from big punishment by them trains, jet planes criss-crossing sky and all. If I had good sense of hearing maybe I even hear cars on the M25 going round and round London. Outside our door, on the lamp post, that stubborn spider is maybe again trying to hang his web across lamp post and the hedge. Inside this house no one go to get broom from the kitchen.

I decide to escape all this and look around Brixton for those graft that you find stuck on window of newsagent and small shop. But when all you see everywhere is 'massage therapist', 'room in flat' and that kind of thing, you can't keep walking on. So me I think I should just relax; if God want to give you graft it will come.

I go check out the salon where Tsitsi is spend all this time selling she baby with MaiMusindo and them other women.

The salon is inside Market Row mall, opposite Elser Cafe. I coil myself at the corner, close to some tramp who have them soldier's eyes. He is drowning his chips in ketchup.

76

In the evening when I tell Tsitsi about that I was at Elser Cafe, she don't like it because she think I'm following she.

'You! Stop following people,' she shout and start to talk about how following people is breaking the law in this country. When I tell she about it, it was just the two of us in the kitchen. I have then go to join Farayi and Aleck thinking that the conversation have finish but she follow me to our room so she can tell me that stalking people is big crime offence. Me I ignore she and try to talk to Aleck and Farayi because it is about 8pm and I have not see Shingi since morning.

Farayi and Aleck is not worried about Shingi.

Them clocks hit 11pm and Shingi is still nowhere to be seen.

In the morning Aleck now start going on like big headmaster telling us how Shingi is not able to take the pressure of Harare North. I want to tell him to be careful how he talk because he have to remember not to get over familiar with Shingi and me because it is not like we have spend our childhood herding cattle with him. I give him one powerful look that is full of skill and he get it.

Farayi, he don't want to get involved in all this so he eat his breakfast hard.

When Aleck and Farayi leave for work, I go to kitchen and make myself porridge. I try to eat it alone in our room. Porridge refuse to go down.

Shingi, I know he will never spend even one night at the old man's place at Tulse Hill Estate, the old man that ran away from Zimbabwe. That old man not going to let that happen. I don't want Shingi to end up becoming one of them people we read about in the papers being found floating with broken umbrellas and dead ducks in River Thames.

I abandon the porridge. Upstairs Tsitsi have wake up for

second time. She normally get wake up by baby some crazy hour in the morning to feed him and then she sleep again. I leave the house because I am not in mood to tune into she talk and songs today.

I have run out of cigarettes and the money to buy them, so before I leave house me I look inside the pockets of Shingi's jacket that is hanging on the nail on the wall and find only seventy-three pence.

I find Tim's Fish Bar. It is this small likkle thing in Stockwell, fifteen minutes' walk from our house and on its glass front Tim have write *Thank Cod For Tim!*. That's where they have graft; one of them 'apply within' things. People that love them fish and chips always coming to this place. Tim is short and well fed, chinless scooter-riding wonder that have barrel stomach that is very taut in familiar way. He also like dog racing. He read the *Sun* newspaper when things is not busy. He is assist by Ricardo, who come from Portugal. But he don't hire me on the first day because he think he can find someone that speak English better than me.

'Can you speak English?' he ask with them arms folded on counter on top of his newspaper.

'Yes.' I also know history and woodwork.

He just want someone that can talk English and is not work-shy. Tim want to know if I have work permit. I tell him I leave it home and he nod with small smile on his face, and say that he want someone that can do the floor cleaning and all other things because him and Ricardo get swamped. I should come back in few days' time. I also have to be sure I can do the working hours, Tim say, and I write these hours inside my head: · 11am to 5.30pm Monday to Friday, or 5.30pm to 11pm Monday to Friday.

I go back home and after three days, Shingi is back into our house from nowhere.

'Why should Aleck and Farayi worry about someone who have relatives in east of London?' That's what Tsitsi say to me as I wash them cold hands in warm water in kitchen sink.

I don't ask Shingi no questions because I don't want him to feel like I'm playing big brother or something on account this might cause clash of feelings and volumes of bad air. If he have decide to visit his relatives, then fine.

I tell Shingi the big story about Tim and his fish bar but he think that I am spinning him one fat old jazz number, I can see in his eyes. He get up from his bed and go to kitchen without no word. Me I follow him. Now he dash around cupboard to cupboard opening door and drawers as if looking for something, giving me them one-word sentences – Hmmm. Good. OK. *Shuwa* – while I am flapping about in the air following his movements in the kitchen.

No . . . now y . . . you will start looking after yourself; that's good because I have no more ginger for looking after some baby that have beard, he say.

Mc I go and sit down on my suitcase and light my cigarette.

Shingi have bring with him some beefsteak that he buy on his way home. He cook some portion only for himself and eat all by himself. Me I just smoke cigarette. He make small talk with Farayi eating and sitting on his bed and I know he have talk about me to his relatives and they have throw some funny mouth around and try to propaganda him against me. That's because he find it hard to save money to send home. All my fault.

Now Aleck come in and start to make fun of Shingi, asking if Shingi is finding pressure of living in Harare North too much because maybe the winds is howling inside him. This thing start

79

as one small joke and even if Shingi not laughing about it, everyone in the house laughing. Then Aleck don't want to drop it and now no one is laughing because it feel funny. One time you is going kak kak kak while someone is being make fun of, and you don't notice the change; suddenly no one laughing any more and all they is doing is just feeling funny and walking out of the room.

'That is not funny,' I tell Aleck straight and square.

When Aleck is gone, Shingi say I can have the last piece of his meat on his plate. But me I don't eat no leftovers. I'm principled man.

'How do you pronounce your name?' Tim ask as he flip through Shingi's passport.

'Shingirirayi.'

'I'm not going to be able to pronounce that.'

'Shingi. Just say Shingi.'

Shingi only let me use his passport and National Insurance number because he want to prove me wrong and show that I can't get graft. But now it's evening and we is all sitting and going yari yari yari about my new graft. Shingi have now start talking more because he also feel good that he let me use his papers to get the graft and now talk as if all this is because of him. Tsitsi is happy for me too. And Farayi, eating soup, is also happy for me. Then Aleck, who have just arrive from work, march into the room to hear what the excite is all about. When I tell him the news he only say, 'Hmmm.' There is small trace of big reasoning on his face. He lean against the door, look at Shingi and start to crack his jokes again, asking if original native and his winds able to take pressure of London.

Farayi pretend he finish his soup and walk away to kitchen. Tsitsi also leave saying she want to go upstairs to put baby to

80

sleep. Shingi just lying in bed with that blank face of some Chipinge cow that have been given away as bride price; he still don't know how to stop people bullying him. Me I decide I don't want to live this funny moment so I disappear too because the last time I stand for Shingi all I get is leftover piece of meat.

10

You see me stepping down them pavements from graft with hands in my pockets and you think you know me? You see me walking from the corner shop with blue plastic bag slung over my shoulder carrying butter, bread, tin of baked beans or sausages and you give me the talking eye that demand your Mars bar? You lick ice cream, I bite mine and you laugh because you think you know my arse better than your mother's petticoat? That's my style that. But that don't matter today because today is not day for styles. Today I have to cry. Today I cry for everything that have happen and everything that have not happen. Today I cry to Mother. I don't know how to cry for she when she leave, Mother. Today I cry because the river of pain have run through our hut sweeping everything with it. Today I cry because the month has end, my patience is now starting to pay. £515 in my pocket; 515 termites in my pocket. Shingi, everything is forgiven.

And this is just beginning of it. Five, six months and I'm out of here if there is no rent to pay. And no food to waste money on. In the dark tailwinds, the footsteps of that news-animal is falling quiet. There's time to pick them termites.

It has been hard. Everything. Even Tim – his accent and cockney thing, you can't hear anything. And when you hear it don't make sense and you have to make your anus tight and listen up to figure things out. Even small things. Like when, after long day, he say, 'I'm cream-crackered.' Or, 'Me knife's going to cut me up if I stay one second longer here.' His knife, that's his wife.

'One for me, one for you.' Shingi and me count the money. You don't get tight-fisted with first salary otherwise the ancestors that have give you all this will take it away. That's how I am brought up.

'One for you, two for me.' It is the first time that we count monies together and that's because me I think he is good friend Shingi. Even if he behave funny when things is hard, me I can understand it because that's how civilians behave sometimes because they is not strong people.

Shingi is filled with heap of happiness as he seat on edge of bed because he know that now he can also buy more time to keep spinning his mama that jazz number that he still have graft in Harare North. I have to make sure things is OK with him now before I start looking for my dollars because he have look after me all this time. I am principled man.

Me and Shingi go shopping. We is talking about what to buy as we walk towards centre of Brixton. Shingi say I need smart corduroy jacket.

It's good idea, me I say. But maybe this time we buy one of them coats with many pockets, you know like the one we see at Oxfam shop last month. This is best time to buy winter things and we can share the coat.

We think it out together and Shingi agree with me. Now we play fight around on them street pavements, jumping on each each's back and nearly fall on someone's shaggy small dog.

We go to Oxfam shop and that coat is still there. It have twelve pockets.

We buy it and now we is feeling like them big tycoons.

Then it's time for food. It's early evening and them streets is still full of people standing outside McDonald's and KFC talking and waiting for they girls like life is one big great street party. We pass one of them crowds when I start hitting the old comrade with them lyrics and plant them ideas inside his head that since he have not find out what it's like to hit front bum, maybe we can try organising sweet sweet time with Tsitsi because this is easy front bum to hit. I see flash of big fright in Shingi's eye. It's the fear of girls that Thoko put inside him at school.

If you leave it too late Aleck will take she back to the auntie and you never see she again, I warn.

I can see in his eyes that he like the idea because he give that boy smile that's full of foolishness and teethies.

Me I'm only joking, I tell him. But she is funny girl.

Shuwa?

Have you not notice?

What?'

She just run around the house pretending she don't know she's big tease. You have not notice?

Shingi say he have notice nothing.

All that rural thing is just one big act, I tell Shingi, but he is silent. Even when I bump my foot on pavement kerb as I follow his big stride trying to tell him I'm only joking.

Me I don't want to do anything to she; I'm five years older than she and I used to be ninja, I crack joke.

She give me them eyes sometimes. But this evening me I don't know that tomorrow I will come back from graft to find Shingi is busy trying to thief his way into she head – sitting on chair like peasant, full of teethies and talking deep kind of Shona while wearing funny shorts and tapping his stump finger on thigh. All that is missing is some hoe for him to lean on and look like he been toiling in humble way all his life, losing fingers and all.

I step inside the house and Tsitsi is in kitchen with Shingi;

he is busy trying to pull them words out of she mouth when she is busy trying to cook. She don't want to talk no more but Shingi is busy bothering she and trying to impress with big Shona words me.

'Tsitsi, *ndeyipi?*' I greet Tsitsi.

'Yes, *kanjani?*' she say.

Shingi, I look him in the eye but we don't say nothing to each each.

I sit on cupboard. Tsitsi is waiting for water to boil when I get my cigarette out.

Tsitsi now have braided hair from the salon women and she look swanky. I fire my cigarette while she wash the pan.

Shingi and me is now just watching she and smoking.

Why you all quiet? she ask.

I'm tired. Hard graft.

Now she hum some song and dash all over kitchen taking things in and out of cupboards and drawers; she is now just swishing she tail around because she know I have come. She know that I am looking.

My head fill up with smoke; now I talk.

Shingi, he is crazy boy, me I shake my head.

Why? Tsitsi shout in she careless rural way.

I just laugh, looking down at my feeties. She is now busy with the baby milk.

He was giving me lesson in how to have sexy time.

Shingi give me puzzled look.

Eiyaaa, Tsitsi laugh.

No, not me and him! He was just talking about how he can make them fancy English girls and they pointy shoes cry if he can get his claws on them.

Tsitsi look shocked and cover she mouth with hand to stop sheself from giggling. Shingi is looking lost.

But he can't even touch them, she say.

I suck my cigarette so there is the small silent moment.

Yea, but he don't really need to touch them. He only have to touch they front bottom and they go howling to the moon, I blow out smoke.

Tsitsi have both hands on she mouth now looking at me like I'm talking things that should not be talked.

He is that kind of boy, Shingi. If I was some father and I catch him in bed with my daughter, me I will tuck them blankets around him to make sure he don't feel cold.

Even Shingi crack up now.

Yes, I tuck them blankets tight like bandage so he can't move one inch. So be careful about having sexy time with Shingi because you go howl to the moon if he touch it.

Stop it, Tsitsi pull serious face.

The water start to boil and Tsitsi turn off gas. She come back and stand leaning against cupboard. She tousle and tousle she braids while we look. Then she turn to window and pretend she now looking at something outside. She is sharp knife.

Now Shingi start again trying to get Tsitsi talking about what songs make she want to do but Tsitsi is not interested no more. He is busy spraying saliva all over as he talk with his hands. Tsitsi not talk; not when I'm here. Me I just fold my arms in front of me while filling my head with more smoke. I don't say nothing.

Now, I say, cutting my quiet, Shingi want Tsitsi and Tsitsi want Shingi. Square square; maybe they must have sweet sweet time? Now, Shingi, this is your chance; get up and lick them pointy breasts and make this thing cry for mercy, I tell comrade.

Tsitsi gasp. Now I can see this look on she face like she not know what to say. At first she have hand over she mouth. Then she start laughing. She just crack up open. She laugh so loud and for so long, Tsitsi. She laugh. Tsitsi laugh. She laugh hard until

Shingi give me this vex cheap face because this thing has put his head out of gear. Tsitsi laugh. Baby wake up and start to cry and Tsitsi run upstairs laughing and not come down until Aleck come back from his graft.

You eat with skill, sleep with skill, graft with skill, and at the end of the month collect your termites. Then soon you is out of here. That's the plan.

Me I'm doing my sums to see how things will work out but this rent problem, like bullfrog, is squatting in the way and looking square into my eyes with its big fat face. I have not finish adding the food bit and the front door fly open. It's Tsitsi. She have heap of surprise all over she face like she have just see Christ cycling through Brixton Market in his kaftan and sandals.

'MaiMusindo have been arrested,' she giggle and put she hand over mouth.

Old spirit MaiMusindo live in Peckham. Last Saturday she have been at our house for the second time to talk to Aleck again about taking the child, Tsitsi, back to she aunt because she's they problem. Now she have been arrest. Tsitsi say they say she get vex and throw one brick into window of neighbour's son's window because he play music too loud and disturb MaiMusindo when she is trying to concentrate on ritual for people who have come to see she.

Everyone in the house go kak kak kak now. MaiMusindo also have crazy rural thing going inside she head. You can tell even when you meet she for the first time. People that know how to fill the air with frightening insults that have teeth, wings and tails – that's they style. But this kind of *jambanja* is the last thing that anyone expect from she.

'What next is she going to do now – pull out some knife on them the police?' Tsitsi laugh.

'She get possessed!' Farayi laugh.

'In the end the police give she £150 fine and big warning,' Tsitsi say as she sit on my suitcase with baby in she arms. She have been biting she fingers and maybe she need set of them nails.

'There is nail bar on Atlantic Road that sell set of twenty-one for £10,' I give Tsitsi hint but she don't get it. I shut up.

'You have full head of hair and you is one hundred per cent sure that tomorrow it turn grey. That's because you see grey heads on the street and figure things out. But pubic hair is different story; it's black now but you don't know if it turn grey, red, pink or blue when you is old. That's because no old codger on Zimmer frame is going to flash they pubic hair to you on the street,' I tell people in the house last night but everyone give me blank face like they don't know what me I am talking about.

Pubic hair is like your future; you have to find out by yourself what colour it become when time has move on. That is true if you are civilian person. But me I am not civilian person. I know how things is going to turn out. I have already pick my second wages. I know the future; I know what the colour of my pubic hair will be tomorrow.

The second month have also been hard work because Tim have been cracking them jokes and I have to laugh even when I don't hear what he is saying because he talk very fast and in funny accent. Sometimes I forget to laugh; his till is always full of money. Ricardo understand Tim sometimes, even if he is Portuguese boy.

Last week I ask Aleck and Shingi if they know what kind of money fish and chip shop can make in a day but they don't know.

Tim, now he is watching the floor spot where I'm cleaning. Soon he is going to start pointing with his finger to show me where the floor is not OK, I know. Tim like to point without talking; that's when he is reading newspaper. He never leave the till, old Tim. But that's OK because it don't bother me. If me I was unprincipled person, all I have to do is wait and then strike. That's because money is like termite; you don't catch it by its head as it try to come out of its hole otherwise it go back and disappear. You just let it come out in the open and soon it is crawling all over the counter. But that's not my style because me I am principled man. You want money – what is better, to try catching it with your own skill and laughter, or to do it by common criminal's way?

Mother's village area is now going to be take over by mining company that belong to commander of armed forces and villagers that don't want to move have been telled that the army and Green Bombers is coming to move them. That's what I read yesterday at Internet cafe. But that is all propaganda because this story is in the *Zimbabwe Independent*, the newspaper that never like our government. What you believe is your best weapon, I know.

And now Tim keep asking me, 'Are you all right?' I am doing my graft and thinking about Mother; I don't know why he hassle me.

Ricardo is doing the frying and don't talk to me much. He don't even do his usual 'Eh *cómo está*, Mr Africa' today.

I spend time washing things and cleaning floor thorough because them Health & Safety inspectors have give Tim big warning about cleanliness matters. Even yesterday, Tim keep trying to give me big cheer cracking them jokes that if he lose his licence he go chop my 'Black & Decker and feed it to the greyhounds at Walthamstow Stadium, mate'.

Black & Decker is cockney for penis, Ricardo tell me.

But now, me I am cleaning them floors, Tim keep asking too many questions when I don't want any question because me I don't know why he want to know so much things about me now and disturb my thinking.

'How is Zimbabwe?'

'OK.'

'How is your family back there?'

'OK.'

'What's Zimbabwe like?'

'OK.'

'How is Mugabe?'

'OK.'

'Are you all right?'

'OK.'

'Do you know what Zimbabwe means?'

Zimbabwe mean house of stone, but me I just shrug my shoulders and say I don't know what it mean because he is hassling me for no reason. Now he start telling me what Zimbabwe mean because he look it up on Internet last week. Me I play dunderhead who don't know nothing. 'It means house of stone,' he say.

I don't want to stay at the fish bar one second longer because me I am tired of watching this man sitting there behind counter and babysitting his machine. Tsitsi is maybe in danger at home, you never know.

I go back to graft and Tim spend whole day trying to break me and make me talk because he want to crack jokes. But because we did not grow up herding cattle together, me I refuse for anyone to break me.

He have pin number for opening that machine, the machine that is turning him into pervert. I have never see grown-up man that have such funny relationship with his machine.

I finish them my duties and have to help Ricardo with unpacking them chips and fish.

Tim have fail to break me. Now he stop teasing me. But you still need crowbar to move him away from his machine.

My shift finish early today. I have just finish packing delivery of them fish into freezer and me I'm walking out of shop like usual when I stick my paw inside my trousers and Tim throw his head up from newspaper on the counter and ask me what I am hiding inside them trousers. Fish bar don't sell no screwdriver if you think I have thief from here. I nearly lick him with the truth but I keep quiet and wait for the truth to come out on its own. Truth is like termite. You just let it come out in the open and soon it is crawling all over the anthill for everyone to see.

'Me I am not thief; I was only turning my tool around because he keep rolling this way and that way, lying on his back instead of lie proper on his stomach.'

11

I don't even have to rush back home today; Tsitsi is going to be late coming home because MaiMusindo have ask she to help. So I don't have to worry who might be touch touching she inside the house. On my way from graft I buy blinding vodka from some Polish rough sleepers on Electric Avenue on account of it is very cold and Aleck don't allow us to switch Farayi's electric heater on because it waste electricity. Vodka is good against the cold. Vodka is good against propaganda.

Aleck is home early when I get to our house. Even if sometimes he give Shingi hard time, I don't mind if he also drink my vodka tonight because I don't want no bad air inside our house.

'Come, we can have drink and be cheerful when we is still alive. Tomorrow we all dead, you know,' I say standing in kitchen doorway and shake vodka bottle to him. He is sitting at kitchen table with his head down eating takeaway food. His mouth is full and he is looking like he is blowing trumpet. I stand by door and wait for him to swallow and lick his lips, but before he have even swallow, he smile, give me the thumbs up and get his head down to the plate again. I know the kind of thing that he was trying to make me feel but he just don't know how to do it right, Aleck. Comrade Mhiripiri know how to do it sweet. He do it to me in first week of learning political orientation and history of the liberation struggle at the Green Bomber camp. I ask if we is going to learn about Mao's Likkle Red Book and he laugh with other commanders and pat me on the head saying we will learn Likkle

92

Red Book when enemy of the state have been scattered and it's time for poems. Look at history, he always say if you push him, the path of many of us is set by few fat bellies with sharp horns and hard hoofs; they gore and trample you the moment they know you see through they cloud of lies. And you think you can fight them with poems? That's his style, Comrade Mhiripiri.

I get into our room and try to whip up cheerful mood in Shingi and Farayi and soon we is having shots. I am not expecting Aleck to come and join us in our room but it don't take long for him to walk in like big man as usual. He want to join in the fun now because we is talking about them Zimbabwean women in Harare North and bawling with big laughter.

'They is getting funny those Zimbabwean girls, especially in Luton; all of them is turning into lesbians or prostitutes *nhayi*,' Farayi say.

'Lesbian? That's just lack of real men; bring them these girls here and we cure this silliness in one night,' I tell him.

Shingi and Farayi roar with laughter. Aleck is still standing like some pole above us and look funny, not knowing what to do and being like district administrator that want to taste the villagers' brew that is passing around in calabash but don't know how to join in the group because he is now big important man.

'You can sit over there, Aleck,' I point to other end of Farayi's mattress. I throw blanket off my shoulders and jump up to go to kitchen to get cup for him.

I pour him one shot, Aleck throw it down his throat in one go and grin looking around at everyone like this is one great feat he have achieve. I grin back and pour him another. Again he chuck it down his throat. This time we clap like you do when some minister has just cut the ribbon to open some new building or something. All of us is all toothy mouths as I pour Master Aleck another.

*   *   *

Alcohol encourage too much joy. You don't let alcohol or joy fill you up too much. That's what Comrade Mhiripiri teach in our training camp. The enemies of the state is always filled with too much joy because the government is having hard time, Comrade Mhiripiri say. But they have no ginger. That's because joy is never good motivator; it stop the vex but it also bury you completely under heaps of self-doubt; soon you is able to see both sides of the story and that get your head all out of gear and then you can't find the fire inside you. That's they biggest weakness them enemies of the state, Comrade Mhiripiri tell us. They don't know how to tie they hearts tight like ball of twine because they is too joyful.

'Guys, things is getting tight. Rent has to go up to £35 per week now. That's including gas and electricity,' Aleck tell us. We don't say nothing but all drink in silence, avoiding each each's eyes and counting our toes.

'*Ma*-face,' Aleck break the silence. 'You know what, I'm craving *sadza nemusoro watsomba* with granadilla Fanta all day.' Aleck laugh to himself. 'And yesterday it was Freezits and rock buns.'

I have never think Aleck is the kind of number whose arse I know inside out. Until now. These kind of yearnings – *sadza nemusoro watsomba* and granadilla Fanta – that's fruit-and-vegetable-vendor-boy diet. Fish head with granadilla Fanta – pure bus-terminus combination. Still that don't say much. But the Freezits? It's the Freezits and rock buns that clinch it. That is true vendor's stuff. *Sadza* and fish head you can say, maybe anyone can eat that. But Freezits and rock buns – no one have those kind of cravings unless you was once part of it the bus-terminus-vending people. Now we have one proper fruit-and-vegetable-vendor boy inside our house. His rope-like, hard dry arms and them calloused hands have all been there before, but I have not see it all this time.

Shingi and me, we have spend big part of school holidays carrying them bags of mangoes and potatoes on our head to sell to them commuters at the bus station so we can earn our school fees. I know what I'm talking about. Aleck like to talk big. Until tonight I have been thinking that maybe he come from proper family, one that don't have to load they children with bags of fruits and vegetables and send them to bus station. We is same same, now it come out.

'So how come you know about Freezits and rock buns?' me I ask Aleck. He get funny. 'Ah, you know, my auntie used to sell them . . .' yep yep yep and all that kind of talk which people do when they have been catch out. Me, Shingi and Farayi just look. Tsitsi have long slip into house quiet and go straight to she room upstairs because Aleck think he is she big brother and don't like she around when we drink because he say she is too young and also that with all she problems, if she get taste of alcohol things go like spaghetti inside she head and she maybe lose it and end up like one of them women that you find on the streets carrying they babies and pulling faces into all kind of crazy triangles outside Tube station.

'And this was not big part of your diet?'

Aleck deny and gulp his vodka, hoping we talk about something else.

Why should we blow incense over fruit-and-vegetable vendor's arse? Me I want to know.

Aleck have big heart, but sometimes he behave like grumpy old school bursar. Before I move into the house, Farayi once fall sick with some terrible bug and everyone is thinking is it the bird flu. But Aleck will not lend him any money to buy medicine. Shingi have no graft at the time and have turn his pockets inside out to give everything towards rent. Farayi cough like chicken and shake under his blankets. Shingi is convince that Farayi going to die, but Aleck don't want to part with one penny because he think Farayi is trying some funny style on him. Farayi don't want to go to the hospital because he have already become illegal, and he only start to get better when Tsitsi, feeling sorry for him, go to buy him some medicine without telling Aleck.

Also Aleck have had run-in with Shingi. It is all because of quarrel over bunch of bruised bananas that district administrator eat thinking that they is going to the bin as they have go so bad he don't think they is fit to be eat by human being, except himself. He learn that he is not the only one who eat rotten fruit when the original native, with big stammer and pointing one spitting mad stump finger at the house rules, demand his bananas back.

Aleck leave our room and we all go kak kak kak into our pillows. Shingi roll on the bed laughing and by accident knock the pile of things that is by his bed on his suitcase. Things scatter all over the floor and this rectangular pack full of them plastic nails fall out into the open. *Halloween Nails* – that's what is written on it in red and black. It's one of them packs that is sold at that nail bar. Shingi rush and bundle it together with other things and throw them inside his suitcase like he don't care about these things, you know this kind of style. Now I know.

Tim have barrel stomach. Ricardo have no barrel stomach but he have got funny exposed throat that stick out bent like chicken throat because of his voice box. That's what I'm thinking. But days push you in waves and soon you is washed off on some new and unfamiliar shore. You want things back to being simple like they was so you can focus on few things only but now you have to tight every muscle because if you don't do that then life collect into one big shapeless thing and soon the whole thing slip off your grasp.

It's all because of them kids that live in estate block near Tim's. Two black boys, one Indian boy and one white girl. They is coming to Tim's more and more now. They get on my nerves because I can't focus now. They come in the afternoon, and sit at one of them two tables and play out they is cool and all.

Now I am cleaning them tables and the floor on other side of counter and they drop in, order chips and sit at the table. They don't eat them chips and just sit there talking and watching me cleaning around. Then, leaving them chips untouched, they run away off cackling and pissing they pants wet.

Tim watch this and don't say nothing because he is breast-feeding the machine. They is laughing at me and he do nothing about it.

Next day they come again and leave the place bawling with laughter. Tim call me to one side and tell me that when I am polishing them salt shakers I should avoid spitting onto the cloth that I use to polish. I listen up but them kids keep coming and doing the same thing. Now Tim tell me that when I am wiping dribble from ketchup and mayonnaise bokkles, I should stop doing it with them my bare fingers because, even if he don't mind, maybe them kids think it's not good hygiene, that is why they is not touching they chips. Tim say I must make sure they have nothing to laugh at and it will all end.

This thing now stretch all the skills inside my head.

I do as Tim say and I stop wiping ketchup with them fingers but them kids don't stop coming. Now they come with two more of they friends and they is laughing all the time and Tim is saying we just leave them alone because they is going to get over it.

'I have do like you say and they is still being funny. Now they is only coming to laugh at me and disturb me?'

No they are not laughing at you; they are only school kids, that's what Tim say. Now he cook up some big excuse saying he don't want to start something because kids like them have to be given respect because maybe they carry small gun.

'I know kids me, if you allow me I can chase them away.'

There is big alarm on his face. 'But they're customers!'

Breastfeeding his machine all the time is getting Tim's head out of gear; he don't understand that them kids is only coming to laugh at me. I give him powerful look and he hold my gaze. This is lot of hard work for this kind of peanut money, I don't tell him. I just leave him propping the counter with his barrel stomach.

In the morning I am lying down on the bed looking into ceiling and trying to weigh options because you can't tell what kind of animal is going to come out of the cloud of news from back home.

Aleck and Farayi have gone to they graft and Shingi is busy doing CV so he can send it to Farayi's employment agency and I have two hours before I start graft at Tim's. Suddenly Tsitsi scream out loud and come running down the stairs. She burst into our room with limp baby in she hands. The baby have vomit blood while asleep and now she don't know if it only pass out or has already dead.

We jump out of bed to look but I don't know what to do with them things like that. Shingi take piece of broken mirror from bathroom and hold it over mouth of baby that Tsitsi have now put down on the bed as she wail. Small steam collect on the mirror. He jump and tell Tsitsi we have to get baby to hospital chop chop. Shingi jump into his clothes and they dash out of house to catch minicab to hospital with whole street looking out of they window on account of big racket that Tsitsi is making as she follow behind Shingi who is now carrying baby.

When we arrive at hospital and them nurses and doctors take away baby on trolley and leave us in some waiting room, Tsitsi now start wailing in proper native way, wrapping them arms around she head and throwing sheself about on the hospital floor in disorderly way and frightening English people. Two nurses have to help Shingi to restrain and calm she down and in the end Shingi is sitting on bench with his arms wrapped tight around she shoulders and head. She have bury she face on Shingi's chest. That's when Shingi whisper to me that people is looking at us funny. 'Maybe you should go away because if you stay around maybe the hospital people start asking too many questions about immigration papers and all,' that's what Shingi say. 'If that happen it put Tsitsi in hard place,' he add.

I can see on his face the style that he is trying to tackle me with; but me I don't make no arguments because it's not good for Tsitsi. I disappear without no word.

12

Moschino Parfum – I see it on one of them vendors' shelf at Brixton Market. I'm on my way to graft but I buy it straight away. £5. That's because yesterday Tsitsi and baby come back home. She have been given heap of papers about how to feed baby healthy diet and also been telled to stop feeding powder milk to baby because that's where they think he catch the salmonella from.

From the market I step off to graft with hands in my pocket.

I get to my graft and I start working my tail off cleaning every surface in Tim's kitchen. I have just start to work on the other side of the counter, doing them two tables with dishcloth, when them kids come in again. I give them powerful look. One of them whisper to others and everyone turn they heads. Suddenly they go kak kak kak.

None of they mothers has ever cook supper for me; I jump for the broom and they scatter out like rats. I go kak kak kak kak.

Tim give me this vex face and jump into this funny style of talk: yari yari yari you can't do that or you get me in trouble with police; yari yari yari maybe if you stop using water in the pail for cleaning tables maybe it will help; it's the same water that you have use to clean the floor yari yari yari.

'Don't just walk away, I haven't finished talking,' Tim shout because I ignore his talk. Ricardo is just holding his head down, hiding his throat, frying his life away and not wanting to get involved.

Tim press some button and his till open; he count money quick, slam the till shut and hold his hand out to give me the money. 'That's it,' he say.

'Me I know about the law now; you can't tell me to go away like so. You have to compensate I know it,' I tell him straight and square.

'OK then. You're fired, mate!' he shout and open till to put back his money.

'Me I'm not going nowhere, daddy,' I tell him and step off into kitchen with hands in my pockets. He look at me funny.

£2,700, that's the number inside my head; I am ready to throw it at him if he want to negotiate.

Now he start trying to confuse me, talking fast and mixing proper English with his cockney and I can't hear even one thing. Me I let rip in Shona and now things is square. That get his head out of gear and he get red like fire extinguisher. Now he start calling police on his mobile phone and spin them long jazz number about how I do threatening behaviour. To prove that me I am peaceful person I leave the place and let the truth come out. Truth is like termite; you don't catch it by its head while it try to come out of its hole or it go back and you don't see it again. I leave it crawling all over Tim's face and I can tell he don't know what to do with it because he is surprised what hole it crawl out of so fast.

'You hungry?' Sekai ask and I say yes. Now she run like animal to get me plate while I smoke my cigarette like big tycoon. That's life. One time you is blue because your plan is sinking just because of big fat white man, then few hours later you have new big chance landing on your lap like them ancestors is looking after you. That's where I am. Sekai and Paul's house.

After leaving Tim's me I did not want to go home or else I end up turning Aleck into bar of soap. And because last week

Paul say I have mail waiting for me to collect at they house, I step off there.

Sekai was shocked to see me and ask me what I want when she open the door. You never ask relative what they want unless your manners is in your pocket, but I don't tell she. I have been knocking on the door for donkey years while she ignore. I don't give up because I know she's there inside; she new car is parked just outside the door.

'Paul is away and I'm busy.' That what she say in short and sharp manner, standing with one hand on the door like she is ready to slam it in my face. But now she is running like animal for me. Things change fast.

'I come to get my letters,' I tell she when and I arrive throwing them glances like there is something behind. Suddenly there is loud bang and she get big fright and turn around forgetting about me. I step inside and the bookshelf that lives in the corridor is face down on the floor and the books is all over. Standing and looking like he had just swallow some wasp was that tall Russian man with small briefcase in his hand and wearing shirt with mismatched button and hole. How he knock down that thing I have no idea because even rhino cannot knock it down.

Sekai's face full of vex and defeat then and all them defiant stares have disappear. She recover from shock and tell Yakov to leave the books alone because she will deal with it. She say it in sharp and vex way; Yakov nearly jump.

She then go inside toilet and lock sheself up leaving me and Yakov looking at each each. He look down at his shoes, he look up at the ceiling in this wooden way, clear his throat but say nothing. He hope that I will say something to make atmosphere easy. Me I say nothing.

I get box of cigarettes out of my pocket, light up and offer him nothing.

He do one short burst of the fast blinking style that Londoners do when they want to avoid eye contact. There is sweat beads on his forehead. He have three long hairs sticking out of his nose, pointing in random directions.

Sekai come out of the toilet and Yakov is relieved. She have puff eyes but better temper. She ask if I remember Yakov and say he have come for cup of tea and I nod my head tight with skill. Things was already shifting my way then.

I look inside lounge, I notice that there has been some big feast, with heaps of food on lounge table.

Sekai say nervous goodbyes to Yakov and me I go sit on the couch. Poor Paul, he don't know that he is pounding front bum that have already been thief by this pointy-headed Rasputin. But life is never fair, me I know. Paul is away in Ireland for few days because of work.

Then Sekai come inside lounge where I was smoking like coal train and she see all this food on the table that she had forget about. I don't refuse it when she offer it to me. That's why now she run like animal to get plate for me. Now she know I am proper relative that have to be respected.

I eat my food silent. I don't say nothing even if I know Sekai want me to say something.

'Get me salt.'

She run, Sekai. You see me stepping down the street with my knock knees and drainpipe-like trousers and you think I am light-weight. But my style weigh as much as hippo, Sekai know now.

She come back with salt shaker and say she have headache so she want to sleep and that I should look for my mail that is in the kitchen.

I don't say nothing. After I finish eating, I collect my letters and shout goodbye from the corridor but there's no reply from they bedroom. I step off to make plan.

* * *

Uncle's letter, this time it say people at Mother's village is being beat up by Green Bombers and police to force them away. Propaganda excuses, that's all this is, I know.

I get to our house and already there is message for me from Sekai on Shingi's phone.

Shingi also want to know when I will buy more food for us; these days I don't waste money because I have to save, otherwise I work for food if I'm not careful. I run to buy tin of baked beans and semolina so Shingi can fill his stomach once.

Sekai. She want to see me 'urgent' at she work tomorrow at the hospital.

She is looking like sharp knife when she come out to meet me, Sekai. She is giving me them funny side looks, all full of smiles like I have never see from Sekai. She drag me to other end of reception hall so we can sit down at table at the coffee bar.

'You OK?' she say after short pointless talk.

'OK.'

'Have you got graft now' she ask.

'Yes. But I have leave.'

She start spinning me this number about how she don't want to hear that I have die of starvation yari yari yari. She is now suddenly talking sweet to me like I am she best friend ever. Me I play along; she is now giving me them Bambi eyes like this is our secret.

'Yes, money have slip away,' I tell she. I can sniff sniff them pounds dropping out of she purse.

In short time we is good best friends because even when she is laughing she now start to throw she head back like she is having good time with my company. Me I bawl into the ceiling like old friend, giving she the high five and people on other tables start to turn they heads wondering what this party is all about.

She dip into she purse and drop me £50. I don't want to throw the number that I didn't get chance to throw at Tim because that will frighten she.

'Drop us £600. Things is tight at our house and me I have to find new accommodation but I have no money to make deposit for the room that I want.'

She blink she eyes at me. Me I tilt my head, you know in that sweet way so she can get the score.

She say '£500,' and get up to run to cash machine outside to get me more while I drink my Fanta.

'Next time you should also remind the Russian doctor that he is the one that should be dropping them pound notes and not you because you is my cousin's wife,' I tell she as we part. 'We have to hit this white man's pocket together until he cry for forgiveness.'

I get back to our house and I am in high spirits and I try to cheer up Shingi and give him the chance to chew my ear about why the long face when Harare North is such great place to live.

By next month me I will be back home, I tell Shingi. Three, four coffee visits to Sekai and I'm on my way.

Bad news for Sekai but that's life; life is never fair, me I have 100 per cent proof inside my suitcase. You think you is frying bean sprouts and suddenly bang, you find yourself frying barbed wire nails.

Shingi is looking worryful now because he have just read letter from his mother, MaiShingi. Things is no more sweet like they used to be because now some bad wind have start blowing inside she house; she husband and his son, Chamu, have whip up bad vibes between each each and now having supper without intervention of riot police has become impossible. Chamu is just being difficult to his father because the old man have no money to send him to Harare North where everyone is going, I tell Shingi. Shingi is lucky because his uncle, Sinyoro, is the one that buy him air ticket. That must make poor Chamu feel like he is left out and now he come with poor excuses for his vex. Even the excuse that Chamu give for the row is poor. It all start when his father decide to go and get membership card for ZANU–PF party because there is food shortage and these days some things you can only get in certain shops that want you to first show your ZANU–PF membership card because they is owned by party people. Chamu now start all this grand talk giving the old man hard time and accuse him of having no morals by carrying ZANU–PF card. But then he eat the food the old man have buy with party card. When things get really heated up Chamu end up moving out of they new house that they have just build on new stand, and he start to survive on thiefing the aluminium street-name plates so he can sell them to coffin makers who use them to make coffin handles. Now the police have catch him and he is languish in remand prison and MaiShingi have no money to get lawyer. I am feeling sorry for Shingi, but then I see it too late that he have herd me into funny corner.

Can I borrow some money? he say.

Now there's funny silence. I want to get out of this situation but I not know what style I have to tackle Shingi with.

Shingi get me vex. I squeeze £500 out of Sekai and six hours later £200 of it have been wired to Harare to save arse of stupid opposition party supporter. This is the same kind of person that the boys have spend long time trying to teach how to think and he still can't come to proper way of thinking. Punishment is the best forgiveness for traitor. That's what Comrade Mhiripiri say. I should never have allow my money to go to bail Chamu. But me I have

106

to keep focus because now I have to make commando-style plan on Sekai and Rasputin. Before the next full moon, I have to be is out of this place.

'All that matter is that we love the baby,' I tell Tsitsi. 'And we don't want him to die of lack of food when we is here.'

Tsitsi don't want to take the money straight out of my hand because she is still snorting and wiping tears, so I put it on cupboard for she to take when she ready. I leave she alone in kitchen and step off to our room to sit on my suitcase again. Things is going bad for Tsitsi. She baby have start growing new teethies and he cry all the time. Tsitsi exhausted by all this and she village madness come out now. She sing careless in the kitchen all alone, with baby on she back, but sometimes she is not singing, and you only notice this when you get close to she. I pick it by accident. That's after I have been trying Sekai's mobile phone dozen times and it keep going to voicemail. I am sitting on my suitcase waiting and I hear Tsitsi singing again.

When I go into kitchen she stop singing. She baby is on she back as she make food for it.

'The rat. I try to kill it but I miss it with that,' she say, pointing to broken broomstick on the cupboard but without looking at it. It's like she want me to do something with the broomstick. She keep she face looking outside kitchen window. When I look proper into she face she swallow hard and I see there is tears in she eyes.

'What's wrong?'

Tsitsi don't talk. The broomstick thing was to stop me coming near she so I don't see she is crying.

She say she don't know any more why she is crying. That's because these days when she cry, even under she blankets at night, she always end up crying about she baby no matter what have cause she to start crying. And she don't know why. But she say she love she baby now, not like when it was newborn when she even look for pit latrine in London so she can throw it away.

'Everything is very hard in here,' she sob. I want to hug and comfort she but you don't want someone to melt into wailing porridge in your hands because then you don't know what to do with that. She have been having hard time with money since baby get ill. That's why I reason quick, go to our room and come back to give she £50.

'I am uncle to the baby now.'

13

'I have run out of money,' Sekai say when on the phone on Saturday morning.

'No worry, me I can wait.' I lay out the whole deal for she to see. 'That's the last time you is ever going to hear from me if you agree to this.'

She is quiet for few seconds. I remind she that Uncle Rasputin will help she. 'Maybe month end will be good,' she squeak.

I am in the kitchen doing my sums. Why we have to pay rent to live inside some hole, me I don't get the score. That can mess up all the sums if you have to wait for Sekai while you is still oozing rent to someone.

Tsitsi. She have go out to them salon women in the morning and now she have come back with MaiMusindo and she tongue in tow. Tsitsi have been borrowing heap of money from MaiMusindo and buying baby things and that kind of stuff because baby is growing teethies and all. Now MaiMusindo have had enough of this because Tsitsi not getting no more money from renting she baby because them council people have blow this scandal into the open. Now Tsitsi can't pay back.

This time there is no big ceremonies and all. MaiMusindo have got trouble all over she face and she just stand in hall like half talisman half crazy thing while Tsitsi call Aleck out of his room. I am coming out of kitchen when Aleck reach stair landing but I just slip into our room without greeting no one because you can tell this is not the time.

MaiMusindo take grand stand on Aleck: my son, in Honde Valley, my rural home where my ancestors' bones is buried, they call me *Nyamutambanengwena*.

Before anyone even know it she have get into gear now in Shona and start to fire: right here, in this house, I can lift my dress up and show you things that will give you bad luck for the rest of your life if you want to try me. Who do you think you fooling? Whose time are you trying to waste?

Now she start shouting.

And this big threat to use sight of she naked body to wither Aleck's eyeballs and turn them into dry figs, that's one big ambush for Aleck who now just freeze on the landing.

She start to list where Aleck have fail, how she try to help Tsitsi but Aleck doing nothing; how the baby go to hospital and she have to give Tsitsi money for medicines; how baby need this and that but Aleck just sitting on his tail.

'My son,' she gasp for air and clear she throat and start another heap of words: oh yeeee you will bawl when your ancestral spirits lay they long stick on you, and you will remember me; them English say you break it you buy it; you have break this child's life; buy it or fix it; you run around saying you is Mr Big Man shop assistant, so what? What good is that if she even too frightened to ask you to help? She is not just like iPod that you keep in your house if it break. You poke poke she, give she this baby and now you deny she, pretend you don't know she and you think no one see? Now you leave she with these problems. What kind of manners is that?

Aleck try to answer but that only give MaiMusindo more fire: oh you have tell me many times what you think. Oh now is my time; if you had keep that front tail inside your trousers none of

110

this will have happen; chop it off if you can't be responsible for what it do.

It's as if with the crack of the whip that is she tongue, MaiMusindo have strike all clothes off our district administrator and leave him naked and cheap like proper vegetable-vendor boy.

'I don't come here another time; don't give me blood pressure oh,' MaiMusindo shout. With that, she put she tongue back inside she mouth and leave everyone reeling from this heavy stuff.

The rest of the day we is whispering and creeping around the house. Aleck lock himself up in his room, Tsitsi remain in she room and I'm with Farayi in our room. When Shingi come, this new stuff blow his socks off. But what blow our underwear clean off is that Farayi have always know this about Aleck and Tsitsi, but like priest, decide to keep lid on dirty stuff. I spend evening putting him on trial for hiding this and want to know what else he know since he is one of them first people to live with Aleck.

'No, there is nothing more.' He lug big frightened eyes like he think Aleck will hear.

Now the problems that Shingi is having with graft and money suddenly looking like child play compared to Aleck's problems. Aleck's mask have come off complete now, and he give Tsitsi big tongue-lashing about the baby's health, why she just don't ask if she need money, how she don't look after the baby proper and why she keep reporting him to MaiMusindo like she's she big aunt when she's madwoman.

Tsitsi is just standing on the stairs holding baby and Aleck is throwing his mouth round and trying to bury she under heaps of bad words. We can hear everything. But Tsitsi now have likkle bit of the stubborn old thing of MaiMusindo; she is steady and talk in calm and unhurried way and this make Aleck get mad because he want to crumple she feathers and don't like it when she answer back. Meanwhile baby is shrieking like this is the end of the world.

Aleck give up on trying to cow Tsitsi and she go to kitchen, wash them dishes and sing old Shona song about bird that don't want to come play because it want to fly high into clouds so it can be like them clouds. Everyone in the house go quiet. Me I don't want to go in the kitchen; you can't trust them girls; they can look strong but the moment they see you walking into the room they want to turn into porridge in your arms and then you won't know what to do with that.

I wake up in the morning after funny dream; maybe it is because of the letter that I write to Comrade Mhiripiri last night when the wind shift inside the house.

The letter, it's still there on my suitcase, less than arm stretch away:

Dear Comrade Commander Mhiripiri,

The ways of thanking great men is as many as there is grains of sand so me I am not even going to try to thank you for everything that you have do for me or we will be here for ever.

Comrade Commander, if what I did back home was wrong, please forgive this son of the soil. I never turn down your help to cause you trouble. Things was closing in on me and you was busy man leaping here and there on every problem that the police and magistrates was causing for me. If police and magistrates cause you more trouble on account of I fail to come with the money, don't harden you heart.

I know things have change now but soon I have to leave this place and plan to land back home next month or so. With them your contacts with important heavy-weight people, if you can please lend a hand. If you cannot, then please point a son of the soil the right way so he can sort things out himself to make sure them those old troubles go away by the time he is back. The money, it's there now.

I remember you, Comrade Commander. I still hear heaps of jazz numbers about you but they all come from people that have turn into traitor.

I remember when you lead us to Buhera, that week when we graduate. That day when we is supposed to sweet them villagers so they go to our party rally. You remember that police roadblock when your great face square up to the great sky and you bark fear with your beard pointing at the policeman that was giving Tom hard time on account of he have no driving licence. 'Enemies of the state is on the loose all over and you is asking about driving licences as if we is civilians?' Your beard point him out and he quickly understand that we have important business to do. You teach us without even talking. As you like to say, fear is like demon; throw it at them and watch. But never let fear stalk you or it end up being overfamiliar with you. Spit on its face. Me I spit on the face of fear now because I am worryful for when I land at the airport home. Help this son of the soil, Comrade Commander.

The funny dream: we is in rural areas for survival training and we have no food and have eat nothing but beer from them villagers that live near training camp. Tom and everyone is raving, talking gibberish and falling over with hunger. Comrade Mhiripiri tell us to think like jackal and find way to get that village food. In the morning we have already make them villagers play game of *tsoro*. Now we come again and they don't understand that this time if

113

you lose while playing with us you have to pay with chicken. In the evening we have heap of them chickens quacking inside cage that is made of twigs and them villagers is not talking no more but giving us talking eyes and walking away because they don't want to play *tsoro* no more. That's when they go inside some hut, get this old man who spend all his days sleeping and they send him to us and he come leaning heavy on his walking stick with gnarled hands and accompanied by small big-eared boy carrying betting chicken. When old man start taking back all them chickens one by one, we have to tell him, 'Ey *makheyi*, it don't matter that you have play this game since before Adam and Eve, but your winning ways is now starting to make us drunk and we don't want to start doling out forgiveness.' He get the score. But then old woman come out of one of them huts shouting like mad and when I look again, it's Mother. She say we should give back all them chickens and learn to give instead of being useless to people in the village all the time. We is leaving empty-handed and I look back at Mother but she face is now Tsitsi's.

Why Mother is so vex with me, I don't know.

Twenty frogs at the well; one jump and go splash up splash down and dead. Nineteen frogs at the well; one jump and go splash up splash down and dead. Eighteen frogs at the well; one jump and go splash up splash down and dead. Seventeen days in Harare North; one jump and go splash up splash down and dead. And then they was sixteen. That's what I'm singing to Shingi as we lie in bed.

W . . . what about f . . . food? That's all he can say.

I am not touching my savings no more now.

And Aleck also want all his rent money. Me I sit tight and wait for month end when Sekai drop us some pounds.

There's bit of food in the kitchen. Aleck and Farayi is homeboys, they is not going to let us starve, is they?

But Shingi shake his head. There has been many big silences in the house and there is funny air since MaiMusindo. And Farayi just want to read his Bible with more fire these days. He don't want to talk.

Shingi is in panic.

The worst thing that can happen is that we owe Aleck bags of money. You owe someone hundred dollars, then it's your problem, but if you owe them million dollars, then it's they problem, you understand? I try to calm him down.

Aleck leave note on our door this morning asking about his rent because the arrears is piling up. Now he come back from his graft and go into kitchen. The next thing I know, we have been command to come and be cross-examined in his court about this rent thing. Shingi lead the way to kitchen; his trousers is coming apart on the seam along his bum crack and I think it have start to look like comedy trousers because the trousers is black and last time Shingi have used white thread to repair the seam.

Aleck have bring some greasy food on his way from work and he is sitting at the table, frowning and looking into this bundle wrapped with grease-stained paper as we come inside and he is doing it in that way that you can tell there is nothing he is looking at there.

'*Mukanya! Ndimi ka munokwira gomo nemamvere.* Four furry creatures on one dead tree at the foot of mountain and the fifth one is right on top of the mountain throwing fruit down to the others; you have look after them poor people, dear *Mukanya*,' Shingi slide in with the oldest style in the book, praise-greeting Aleck and elevating his totem – the baboon – to tip-top mountain heights. Aleck give poker face. He poke poke his greasy bundle pretending we is not there.

Shingi quickly rescue us all from this funny situation and go straight to the matter. Now Aleck snap back into grand voice. 'Final warning. If you can't pay in two weeks' time you have to make new accommodation plans,' he kick hardball.

We is leaning against them cupboards and short of answers. Does Aleck know that he can be charged for statutory rape for what he do to Tsitsi? I want to ask Shingi. You have to earn right to make harsh judgement on anyone in this house; it don't just land on your lap like banana from your mother. If you have been raping small girls then all your rights is gone.

'So when do you think you can pay?' Aleck ask.

Shingi and I give each each them glances. Sweat beads is already forming on Shingi's nose. Aleck is munching loud. His mouth is full.

'You really looking for graft?' he ask and his eyebrow jump up.

'Y . . . yes yes, I try my best. But you know how things can be in . . .' I say.

'How come you lose your last graft?' His lopsided mouth pull his face to one side.

A week has not even go splash up and splash down dead and Shingi is salad-picking in Stanford-le-Hope, being drive from Barking in minibus every morning by them the usual bullet-headed boys with spotty faces. Me I don't really want graft now. I have put enough Mars bars inside pockets of them these gang-masters, I tell Shingi. Me I now only wait for Sekai's month end.

Shingi give me the long face but I don't want to listen to him otherwise he will make me change my mind.

We wake in the morning and our pillows is still wet from all them tears laughing from last night. Farayi haul the news into our room last night when he come back from weekend visit to old friend in Luton. Aleck is now two times naked.

We have give him hard time before about him hiding secrets about Aleck, and last night Farayi want to make up for it. The moment he step into our room we can tell that he is excite by something because his bundle of bum is flying loose all over the place and his neck is sunk deep into his shoulders like he is mischief priest that is about to say naughty thing.

'Farayi, *ndeyipi*?' I say.

'Ah, nothing.' Farayi put on this ask-me-ask-me style on his face. So why let the bum jump jump all over like that?

'H . . . how is the ho-homeboys and homegirls in Luton?' Shingi jump in.

'Tight tight; they is staring at fire; living rough.'

'What's the news?'

'Now, the serious news . . .' Farayi sigh with big grin on his face. He have now lie down on his bed and his legs is kicking with excite like he is trying to swim. 'You promise not to tell anyone, please?'

'No nooooooo!'

Farayi is trying to make us promise all sorts of silly things and we is getting tired of this when he spit it out.

'I meet someone who know Aleck. He says he is not shop manager like he tell us.'

'What then?'

'Eh, that I can't tell.'

'Y . . . you m . . . might as well have not tell us nothing.'

Your psalm-singing buttocks have nothing to say.

Farayi kick his legs on his pillow with more fire. Shingi get up like he is going to toilet and have no more ginger for this.

'OK, now shhhh.' Farayi put his finger on his lips.

'Yes?'

117

'They say Aleck actually work as BBC in Croydon.'

'Kak kak kak kak,' Shingi let rip as dive onto the bed and bury his face into our pillows.

'Aleck picking old people's *kaka* off beds and then coming here walking around like he is district administrator coming every time to collect tax money even when we have nothing. Harare North is funny place; you put them Mars bars inside pockets of people that is proper citizens and you also have to put Mars bars inside pocket of some BBC while you is struggling to get back home in time. Things that is visited upon us in Harare North . . .'

We laugh throughout the night until our ribs is sore, and Farayi now open up and start talking about this guy that know Aleck because they was working together in Croydon. He leave because they was being exploit because they don't have work permit.

14

Sekai go to Zimbabwe yesterday, that's what Paul say. She brother have throw himself down from eighth-floor balcony and dead.

'Have you read the news about what is happening at your Mother's village?' he ask.

'I don't want to hear no more of this propaganda. I have read everything and I know what to believe.' I hang up on his arse.

Just because Sekai has go away, me I don't go *paparapapara* panicking like chicken or civilian person.

Shingi come from salad-picking and make big cry about how the work is killing him and how he hate having to get up at 4.30 in the morning every day. Aleck panic thinking that now Shingi want to stop graft, and he demand that we pay all the rent for the month ahead.

Someone is going to make fearful leaps inside this house as I turn him into one bar of soap. Me I'm not touching my savings now.

Saturday morning. We is going kak kak kak kak into our pillows again. This is funny. None of us have ever take holiday to reason proper and put Aleck and this house under microscope. Truth has always been inside the hole. Now it have come crawling out into the open without us ever looking for it.

He have spin us this jazz number before about how the house owner ask him to look after it because they go travelling but we have never reason it hard because there's too many thoughts raving and screaming inside our heads and we have to discipline them to survive.

You can never tell when things is about to change; the morning start not so bad. Shingi get letter from relative in Chipinge and he is reading it while I sit on my suitcase smoking my cigarette. Cloud of blue tobacco smoke hang silent in the air around me like time is refusing to shift. The mischief priest, Farayi, is taking shower; Aleck is still in bed. And Tsitsi, after waking up early because of crying baby, have now go back to sleep. The house is quiet.

Then Shingi go out of the house for walk because the letter make him worryful. He come back one hour later hauling bag of skunk that he pick from skip. Shingi is expect me to jump and shout but by then me and Farayi have already see the termite and nothing interest us more than this. Aleck is still in bed then and have not yet see his mail. There is this postcard card for him with Indian stamp. It is from Mirjam and Ed and they is saying how, even after two years away, they don't know when they is going to be back in England and that if Aleck want to move out of squat he should email them so they find someone they trust to take over.

Aleck is lucky boy, Farayi talk. When he come to England Aleck is one of them people that also get the visitor's visa and on arrival pull the fast style on the Immigration Department, claiming asylum. But he get refused asylum and join activist group that is campaigning for Zimbabwe asylum seekers and they spend they time dancing and waving they placards outside Home Office building. That's where he meet this Mirjam and Ed couple who was squatting in the house, and when they decide to go to India, Aleck is living rough and so they leave the squat to him. Now Aleck jump into it and start to invite them natives, whipping £35 per week out of them when the English people have leave the squat to him for free. And now he is busy making money and buying them stands back home.

'So this is squat? Did you know?' I ask Farayi and he sing the usual chorus of yari yari yari I have tell you everything.

Hmmm, F . . . Farayi know th . . . the score all along, Shingi laugh.

'No, nooooo!'

'Don't worry, we not going to throw you in bonfire.'

Me I light small bit from the skunk pillow that Shingi pick. He is also puffing smoke and it's coming out of every hole on his body. Smoke fill the whole place and before long we have smoke the mischief priest out of our room because he think skunk is evil. That's when Aleck wake up and come down to tell us that we stop it because we is filling the whole house with smoke. We stub out without even throwing one bad word.

'It's not like we have break into his family house and thief his mother's petticoat; what's his problem?' My head is full of smoke now.

'Oh, Minister Zvobgo is dead.' That's the kind of mouth Aleck throw in careless style. He have spent all of this week reminding us about the rent that we still owe him. Me I am now getting tired of knowing that he is going to keep hitting our pocket until the return of the Messiah. I don't want to get eaten with my eyes wide open as if I am sardine.

Now he start this yari yari yari: yeee it's only the good people that die while Lucifer himself not die; yari yari yari even death is getting disorient by size of Mugabe's evil.

After spending the afternoon hitting Shingi's skunk, me I have funny light-headed feeling now. JCB bulldozers can clear any village, I have been reasoning. Anyone's village.

In the sky the moon tremble through the window and make

121

me feel like I don't belong to earth. Sekai is taking for ever to come back from Zimbabwe, Shingi is not talking and Farayi is reading the paper hard like smoke is soon going to start coming off them newspaper pages. No one is talking. Except BBC boy.

'Shingi, you are Chipinge man; do your rituals, strike the earth with knobkerrie and talk to your ancestral spirits and see what they can do about Mugabe,' BBC boy cry as he pace up and down in our room like district administrator.

Shingi grin like fool. He always say he have no opinion on these matters about the president.

Sitting on my suitcase me I flick through my new pack of cards and shiver like the winds. My skin look like that of chicken but I'm not chicken. Aleck give me them looks like he want to start me.

'Why you looking at me like that; do I remind you of your mother?' I take grand stand on him. There is sharp look of surprise on his face because he think that, like Shingi, I also have no opinion about the president.

'You should not go around making big talk about things that you has likkle knowledge of,' I add, shuffling them cards and trying to find my stride.

Aleck recover, fold his arms, shift his weight to one leg in fancy homosexual kind of way, fidget above me before he fold his arms and support his chin on one hand as if to he is saying, 'Here we go again, let's hear what you have to say this time.'

'You so sure you know Bob well enough to judge him. Do you know anything about ZANU–PF?' I ask putting my cards on the floorboards.

Aleck tut-tut and shake his head and laugh at me: yeee you are just one big ZANU believer; yeee you have been brainwash too much by ZANU; yeee stop bigging up that that tired old fart!

He have forget that me I can give one powerful look.

122

'You call me ZANU believer? And you, have you not been brainwash?' I challenge him but Aleck is just in screaming mood: yeee it's not big secret; it's not hidden; yeee go back home if you have forgot what your Bob is doing; people getting clubbed, women raped, people's houses getting burnt; what is all that?

He hold his hands open up in the air, like you know, he have win.

'Who has ever see Bob walk around setting fire on them people's roofs or raping women?' I ask.

Now he go into big sermon about how me is not reasonable; Mugabe is evil dictator; it's always the case with them African presidents; they don't know when to leave power; yeee what has he done for you or your family?

Now this is getting out of order; I have to hit this head with one stone-question to get it out of gear and let all the oil drain away.

'Me I want to know what give some BBC the right to dismiss them presidents of one whole continent just like that?'

Aleck have not expect the termite to come out crawling all over his face so quick and in front of everyone.

'Eh . . . e . . . but . . .' he stumble and blink like lost goat. 'You know . . . you know,' now he try to talk in English, but I already find my footing now.

'You have small knowledge of them African presidents that you is jumping to dismiss. Even all this style of treating us like we is evil or something just because we have no rent money is silly games. This is just squat. We all have hear of some witch who take off in one direction or another screaming and pretending to be terrified of small lizard when underneath they drapery she have black mamba tied around she waist. Show us your waist, Aleck.'

Tsitsi, who have just walk in, laugh.

'Shingi, look . . .' Aleck now he try to appeal to Shingi for support but I don't give him no space.

123

'I've seen them kind of people, Aleck, and these is the same people that go around spreading them lies about Bob. Some of us is here not because we want to spin jazz tunes and have few crumbs of bread dusted our way by them white people. Neither is we in Harare North to wipe they bottoms. And everyone know that this place is squat; them walls have eyes, ears and mouth and they tell. We supposed to pay rent for this hole? Answer yes or no, Aleck.'

'I . . . I agree with Mirjam that –'

'No, answer yes or no!'

'But –'

'Answer yes or no, Aleck!'

Now, there is silence in the room. Aleck's mind go blank and he just look at me with long cheap face.

'TKO!' I blow smoke into the air.

The conversation should have end there, but Aleck have paranoia and decide to quietly settle down on Farayi's bed looking broken and hoping that his presence will stop us from tilling his back if he leave the room. He is hoping that the mention of bum wiping will be quickly forget so that he can leave without have to worry about his back.

'Fine. Maybe you think Bob is evil but that's just your opinion.' I leave the rent problem now because I have win that one clean. 'And that's all it is. Mine is not just opinion; I earn it. I earn it through what I have see, I earn it through what I know now. And you will never know who I am unless you have also been where I have been. Never. Me; me I don't allow myself to be given lecture by them people who, while life was tossing me about like some straw, they was flicking *rapoko* grain at they grandfather's beard and listening to them old fables and old jazz numbers. You see me hiding under the same roof as you and you think that we is all the same folk. Me? Me and you being same same? Nooo, Aleck! Some of us have defend the country from them enemies of the state who have break loose inside house of stones. Yes! Those people that everyone despise; the Green Bombers; the boys of the jackal breed; the boys that drink beer instead of tea for breakfast; they know them things that BBCs don't know,' I say, my head now getting into fifth gear.

Now Tsitsi laugh. 'Heeee heeeee what is it that you people do to him?' she ask.

In them other housemates' eyes I see black-eyed fear.

'What country did you defend?' Tsitsi giggle with she hand over she mouth. Farayi, on his bed, is hiding behind his paper pretending he is not there. Aleck, broken, is now picking fluff off Farayi's blankets in absent-minded way. Me I turn around and get another joint from under them pile of blankets that is my pillow.

'I want to know, honest,' Tsitsi is laughing.

Me I light my joint and ignore she.

Aleck suddenly get up and shoot out of room without warning. Everyone fall quiet but I don't worry. 'If he is not careful he is just asking for heap forgiveness now.'

Then Shingi also go funny because he is upset that I have now bring my Green Bomber past out into the open.

The evening end with Shingi in headache kind of mood which he hang onto for rest of the week. At the end of that, for the first time ever, Tsitsi run away from she room upstairs because she say she is also scared Aleck is in funny mood and will do something to baby. It's all because of quarrel between them, with him accusing she of having no conscience when it come to using margarine, especially when she is not bring much money in.

Shingi say I should not get involved.

Me I am tired of Shingi not wanting to support me. Everything I have do since coming to the house is to support him and try to stop Aleck giving him hard time.

If you want to be with Aleck that's fine, but me I am on Tsitsi's side if Aleck try to toss she about; she is mother, Tsitsi, and don't need useless people around she, I tell Shingi straight and square. Aleck, all he have do is thief all our money pretending he is landlord, I tell Shingi. 'If it was not for this silly rent me I would be back home years ago.'

Shingi don't like straight talk so he go into headache mood again and do his disappearing thing.

The day end with Aleck and Tsitsi making up. I know that if Shingi was around he will have say usual silly wise thing like, 'See, I tell you not to get involved and you don't listen . . .'

15

I wake up in the morning. The air in the house feel funny. People don't like living under same roof as Green Bomber. I don't feel like staying inside this house.

The sun have come out of nowhere to chase big fat mama clouds from the sky – just when spring is beginning. And Sekai have already spend a decade in Zimbabwe and is still nowhere to be seen. It is one of them warm days that make them unusual people crawl out of them Brixton's houses and into the streets in big numbers.

I go to Ritzy Cinema. Under the big chestnut tree. There is heap of them laid-back liars, dog thieves in trenchcoats, pigeons, coarse runaway married men that have develop bad habits like spitting on pavement every minute, them the crazy ones and them the ex-pig keepers who have flee they crazy countrymen in hot climates; all them funny types is gathered there on the grass or the benches.

With hands in my pockets, I sit on bench. That old man from Tulse Hill Estate, the one that don't like being known by home-boys, he is there wearing cap and brown oversized dungarees, blue long-sleeved shirt and old boots. He have reinvent himself complete; you will never think he is Zimbabwean if you don't know him. Now he is busy sucking cigarette, blowing them great clouds of smoke while everyone sit around him, hanging on every word he talk.

In foreign place, sometimes you see each each with different eyes for the first time and who you are and your place in the world suddenly become as easy to see as any goat's tail. Sometimes people don't like it if they think you can see how far they have fall. If he don't want to be known, that's OK with me. Last week I meet him in Brixton Market and he give that air, you know, that kind of smell someone throw off when they don't want to talk to you too much.

Now he have old dartboard beside him. I can already sniff sniff that this is the kind of homeboy that can visit Germany for one week and come back to his native country putting on big funny American accent and spinning clouds of jazz numbers playing out he don't understand his native language. He have change completely.

I light my cigarette.

'His name is the MFH – Master of Foxhounds,' Khalid say and I give him one cigarette. Khalid have just come to sit next to me without being invite. He is Somali boy and have bleeding nose because have just been involved in fight but he get mauled. Someone is still talking about how Khalid start fights but always lose.

Khalid swig brandy and start to shoot off about how the old man say he is American with many degrees; one in psychology, another in science, computers, crime, the climate – just about everything. I know this kind of style.

Near the MFH, Peter who is Ugandan boy, is claiming to have desert the Ugandan army in 1991 and can't go back home. He have his head dangling to one side, dancing and singing. 'When I'm in Uganda, dancing like this, holding my AK47 like this!' he sing and leap around with them arms fold to his chest as if he hold baby. Everyone is quiet and watch. Even Oliver, the junkie and dog thief who lie on bench with greasy bunch of blond hair hanging to the ground, he have stop telling everyone that bus drivers no longer hassle him because his smack dealer, who prefer dealing on the buses instead of them streets, spit on one of them drivers' face.

Some tramp with bent cigarette in his mouth and wearing socks only – one with big hole on heel – stand up from among them ranks, stagger past me, scratch his head, take his cap off, twist his face in reckless way and challenge the MFH. 'Today I beat you at your own game, mate. Five smackers I bet!'

Everyone look. The MFH is taken aback. 'Who are you?' he ask, eyeing the man from toe to head like he suspect this is set-up. The man say he want the MFH to bet five smackers. 'Are you scared?' he ask.

On them faces of everyone around there's gleeful looks. Someone rush and grab dartboard from the MFH and hang it on the chestnut tree. Peter come and stand between the challenger with no name and the MFH, ask them to put them fivers each for him to hold and give to the one who win. The MFH look like he is not interested because he don't think this is serious challenge. The man with no name stagger and search his pockets and only manage to come out with coins that add up to something like £3. The MFH wave the man away like he have no time for this. Me I light another cigarette and step off. He have change.

16

I eat Farayi's baked beans without no permission and Aleck try to expose me as thief. I have break them house rules, he say. But I only eat Farayi's beans because I know that I will replace it soon. Farayi don't complain; he just keep quiet because he is nice man. But Aleck, me I don't get the score with his problem.

It's two weeks since Shingi disappear now and another margarine quarrel start between Tsitsi and Aleck. This time Aleck is accusing Tsitsi of being heavy-handed and spiteful with the way she use the sugar and milk.

Me I decide maybe I fill my time by fixings things that Shingi pick from the skips and put in back garden. I can't just watch all this shouting; I have to do something that involve skill to take my mind away from this.

I get my screwdriver and start tightening loose screws on them old computers and whistling to myself thinking how there must also be lot of loose things inside this house.

Tsitsi again desert she room upstairs because she is frighten Aleck will do something to baby. Now things is moving faster than dog with ten legs, you can tell. That's because out of the blue Aleck come from work full of them blues and threaten to beat the poo out of Tsitsi. He say it's because she fail to cook for him proper when he work so hard and she spend day grazing the food off them shelves and then running off to tell on him to MaiMusindo. But there is nothing that I can do if the quarrel is only about food. Now Tsitsi come to sleep with us downstairs.

I give up my bed for she and sleep on the floor. I don't touch she. She can turn into porridge or into your mother in your hands and then what do you do with that?

Aleck get vex by this move. In the morning he give me long stupid looks. When he leave for graft, me I hit his sausages and leave nothing in the fridge.

He come back from work in the evening and lash out at Tsitsi for wasting them sausages to fatten sheself. When I tell him that it is me that hit them sausages he chill with big speed. He don't even apologise to Tsitsi, and maybe now Tsitsi also start to have the battered-wife kind of thinking because I am left feeling cheap and stupid when they make up and he apologise and promise to take she to she aunt next week. She move back upstairs. What kind of mother is this?

No sooner have Tsitsi move back than Aleck start throwing them tantrums again. He come back from work looking like he have not sleep for twelve donkey years. This time he accuse she of not looking after baby proper because the thing have been crying all night and Aleck don't get no sleep in his room. Farayi have not yet come back from work that evening and me I am the only other person at home when this is happening. There is nothing that I can do. Even when he push she on the face and send she tumbling backward down them steps. I walk out of this house and spend hours wandering through nowhere and everywhere and with unlit cigarette hanging from my mouth because I even forget to light it.

Tsitsi and baby move downstairs again. And again in the morning Aleck give me funny look. When he leave for graft, me I hit all the bread that he have buy the day before.

He come back from work and scream himself hoarse calling me

dunderhead pig because I don't have no O levels like him. I don't say one word.

Tsitsi is now crying all the time. Then he try to drag Tsitsi upstairs. That's when I put my foot down. 'If you as much as touch she again, you can expect some very sweet tender loving caress from me. And heaps of forgiveness. You don't do that to mother,' I warn him.

Shingi is back in the evening. Farayi also don't want to have anything to do with all this what is going on.

The kind of thing that Aleck have been doing – he should not complain if Zimbabwean community in Harare North start throwing funny kind of mouth around, I tell Shingi. I am now sleeping on the floor because I have offer the bed that we was sharing to Tsitsi and baby.

Shingi is worryful about what is happening. That night he sleep on floor with me but he have big stress about Aleck who have lock himself up in his room and don't want to talk to no one.

In the morning, Friday, when Aleck and Farayi have leave for graft, Shingi now spin me some jazz number about how he just want to take walk. He have been so worryful last night he even forget to tell me that he have lose his salad graft.

Everyone is away all day, me I give my mouth permission to hit everything that was buy by Aleck in the kitchen. I tell Tsitsi that she can share food with us. Shingi is back and he have bit of money. Me I have to be careful with my savings now.

Aleck arrive from work and do the most dunderhead thing, coming straight on me with them flying fists and all. I dodge his girlie jab and, in one styleful and thief-like ninja move, I sock him straight on the mouth. He tumble on the floorboard, pick himself up and run upstairs with speed of animal with ten legs, spitting bloodied tooth. He is now in trouble, Aleck; ancestral spirits is giving him heap of forgiveness with long stick, MaiMusindo warn him. Me I am heavyweight spirit, he should know.

Shingi roll back into the house at midnight and everyone have go to bed. Me I am still awake in the dark room but I don't want to start talk about what have happen because Shingi maybe start to get worryful and all that kind of regular civilian people's style.

In the morning we wake up and Aleck is gone. Just like that. Tsitsi is first to discover that Aleck have leave the squat. London is breathing into his room through them open window, sending copies of the *Metro* and many other papers flapping about. We all take looks into deserted room and quickly go downstairs to our room. None of us need explanation what this mean. All Aleck have to do is to stop at nearest phone box, call them police and tell them about nest of them illegals who is occupy this house. Then he simply jump into sea of 10 million Londoners.

Without one word, I pack my suitcase and make my way to the chestnut tree, where I sit and smoke cigarette. Shingi is not happy, but he come with me having realise that even if he is not illegal, the police still able to bag him if it turn out something is unlawful about the squat. I have tell Tsitsi that because she have baby and she is just likkle girl, she don't come with us but maybe go to MaiMusindo.

Shingi – I can tell from the look on his face that he blame me for everything. He is quiet and it's like I am big headache for him. We sit for long time without exchange of word.

Them chestnut-tree people have not yet arrive. As Brixton people get out of they beds inside they warm houses we sit silent.

Tsitsi is still gathering she things inside the house. Me I am worried that them police will find she, but soon we see she shuffling down Acre Lane and cross Brixton Road to go to the hair salon with baby on she back. We watch she crossing the road at the traffic lights outside McDonald's and then go down Coldharbour Lane.

Then them homeless people start to trickle to the tree with they dogs, ready to start to put out the burning truths of they lives with buckets of brew and all.

17

We spend the morning sitting under the tree, but by about afternoon Shingi maybe relax or feel pity for me.

He wave olive branch and start talking about where we is going
to spend the night. I have been whipping them pounds out of
Sekai and she have now decide to take few more weeks off in
Zimbabwe. I don't want to go sleep at they house and spend time
with Paul.

Shingi don't want to go to his relatives and leave me alone in
them streets.

If I t . . . take you to m . . . my relatives they is not going to
be happy, he say. Maybe I s . . . stay with you for the night and
then we s . . . see.'

I have also help him in the past when he don't have graft and
his family have him on the ropes about money issues while he try
to spin jazz number of having graft.

You are kind man, I say to him. We is back on talking terms.
He don't want to take me to his relatives because they already
propaganda against me, I know.

'Where are you from?' It's this man that have Karl Marx's beard.
He sit cross-legged and hunch over his left arm while the other
hand stroke his beard. He have siphon part of his beard into his
mouth and is chewing. Our eyes clash and me I look away.

Under the tree, sitting opposite me is three faces. Three faces
and they two dogs. They sit silent on low brick wall that border

the lawn area, each wait for his turn to take swig from bokkle that is doing the rounds. Some few steps to they right is three dread-locked Rasta faces, one of them try to cheer them up, hobbling around and singing and shaking them mangled dreads. Karl Marx at the corner of wall to the left of them three faces and they dogs. I don't want to answer questions from no one right now. He get the score without me saying one word.

Shingi come back to the tree with flyers for free concert called 'African Guitar Virtuosos' or something at Southbank. I tell him we should just start heading to Southbank because me I don't want staying here with this Karl Marx guy. But before we step away I go and check in military style if any police is already crawling all over our house. The house look deserted. It look at me with them sad eyes, this Shingi's head. No sign of police yet but me I am not stepping inside that head. Not today. I go back to the chestnut tree and we step off to Southbank.

Bada nepakati, Shingi instruct me. With both hands me I hold the loaf that he buy from supermarket. I pull and it tear in half. Shingi grin in nervous way and he look at them people around us. The bus is full and everyone on the bus point they eyes at us.

I apply myself on the bread. This feeling that I have not have in years now come over me; my senses get more fire. I clutch the half loaf between them arm and ribs, and rip into it with them fingernails. The warmth of bread against my body, together with it the happiness of discover the freedom to tear down loaf of bread on London bus, send message of goodwill to my bones. I feel free.

Then out of the blue sky we get ourselves some fan: one small plump boy sitting with his mother leap to his feet with big eyes. He wear T-shirt written 'Made Of Money'. Shingi have good talent at reading them people so he see quick that likkle boy Made

136

Of Money is in grip of big hunger. He break small piece from his bread and stretch out in that good-old-uncle kind of way, and hand it to the likkle man. The look of horror on the likkle boy's mother's face can kill a hippo. She look on but she is helpless. I can see that she want to stop she son from taking the bread but hold sheself back because she is frightened of the racialism thing. She remain on she seat, and only watch with sickly smile as she son hit the bread with more fire.

Southbank is crawling with them Africans in they colourful ethnic clothes it make you feel like you is not African enough. Many of them is also them lapsed Africans because they have live in London from the time when it was OK to kill kings, queens and pigs. You can tell because they carry smiles like they have take over the palaces at last. We is only one wearing jeans. But this is make up for by the fact that after the concert we have good cheerful smiles because of the one person who have had the sense not to lumber himself with them ethnic things. That's the original native from Kinshasa.

The guitar men step onto the stage. Three of them. All of them is dressed in flashy African clothes except for him the Kinshasa boy. The other two guitarists is just lapsed Africans, but they is busy spinning clouds of jazz numbers that they is Tanzanian and Cameroonian and whatever they can think of. But the worst is him the one that want to be Cameroonian; he change his costume three times during the show. Three times, I count it. Even girls don't do that.

Cameroonian man twang away while his Tanzanian friend is busy ripping away them lines off his guitar. But the original native – he is dressed in jacket and tie and is sitting onstage like lost schoolboy. Even when he was introduce at the start of the show he look like he have heaps of confusion on his face, you know like what it's like when the native have just hit Harare North.

Kinshasa boy wear black oversize jacket and them baggy grey trousers; you can tell these is clothes that he is suppose to have taken to dry-cleaner but maybe somewhere in the township the original native decide that this is something that he can handle with box of Surf powder and bucket of water; now they is puckered and getting all out of shape in that way that make them more African than them thousand cotton garments with blue lizards, green fish and ethnic patterns. This cheer our face.

Shingi, he have big grin ripping through his face right up to them back teeth. The music crackle away like rhythm of them hoofs of herd of donkeys at full-speed gallop. Shingi's attention is fix on Kinshasa boy, who is looking at them the other guitar men with mix of shyness and absent-minded style that often hide native impatience. He tag along nowhere near his limit while them other two is at full gallop.

Suddenly something snap inside his head and Kinshasa boy get off his stool. From the way the hairs on my back stand on they ends, you know that now something is in the air. He throw left leg forward in that playful way like he say, catch it if you can. But this is that style that is awkward by purpose, you know them those crazy 'I don't care' ape-style *ndombolo* moves. He step and sway. He peep. At you. Sometimes.

Kinshasa boy. He do sharp feint. He sway and step. Bobbing head. Phantom step; he almost shake. One jink, and he send the whole audience swaying the wrong way. Then it come one deadly sideways leap of the eyebrow that kill all the xenophobia, hippopotomonstrosesquippedaliophobia and yugoslavia that exist in London.

His trousers, they flap mad. Like some flag in middle of big storm. Now he cling to his guitar with more fire and hit the crowd with heap of notes that come out faster than light machine gun.

'My friend, you, civilian person like you, if you is not careful you will drop small poo in your pants because of this pleasure,' me I tell the man sitting next to me with high-wattage grin on his face.

Even them, the other guitarists, is now just onlookers like us. And when Kinshasa native start to get down to stepping on the rhythm with some mental *ndombolo* footwork, whipping his own back with them hot riffs, too many truths that cannot be named crawl out of they holes and start crawling everywhere. Me I nearly throw £50 onto the stage but Shingi hold me back.

When the show end, the whole concert hall is crawling with termites you don't even know where to put your foot.

After Southbank we hang out at Trafalgar Square for the night. We wake up late morning and decide that maybe we check what happening in our house. If it come to the worst, at least the police is not like Zimbabwe police; here they call you 'sir' instead of 'thief' before they start touch touching you.

Some ghetto bird start hovering and chopping the air in the sky above when we jump out of bus in Brixton.

'Is this another case of police chasing prisoner that have escape from Brixton Prison or what?'

Shingi say nothing. He is staring at this teenage boy leaning against scaffold on his bike outside Woolworths. The skunk smile on his face is like he is laughing at us carrying our things.

We go and stand at the corner outside KFC. You can see things better here – down Coldharbour Lane, up Acre Lane, down Brixton Road, up Effra Road and up in the sky. But Brixton is funny place this afternoon. You can just see it when you look around. Them, the street vendors, skunk dealers, the incense vendors, Tube ticket touts, homeless people and thiefs. I don't trust no one here.

'Repent! Repent! Humble yourself because the Second Coming

of the Lord is as sure as the First!' one man cry. He is speaking to us.

'. . . He says he doesn't like his brother, but he loves the Lord Jesus?' He raise his Bible up in the air as if he expect someone from the crowd to respond. Then he slam it into his left hand to emphasise, 'Do not be deceived. Do not let the Devil deceive you, my brothers and sisters!'

Before we know it two police is upon us; fat man and thin wire-like woman.

Relax, think like e . . . e . . . everything is normal; p . . . put the suitcase down and relax.

We is outside KFC where it's full of teenagers that loiter in they hoodies, bling-bling and wanting heap of respect. Them officers is a few steps away and walking towards us.

'You behaving yourself, Jay?' the policewoman ask with likkle smile as they walk past them teenagers.

'Yes, officer, I am good these days,' the boy answer in proper English now.

'It was just ghetto behaviour, it's tribal,' someone laugh.

Them officers walk past. They don't say nothing to us.

You never know if the police have play people's mouths and get information about you. The whole afternoon we run around to corners and don't want to talk to no one. When the sun go splash down dead, we put on bold face and step easy easy to our road. It's quiet and there's no sign of funny thing. The house with its nose and them big eyes look at us. We forget to switch off the lights when we run away; they is now shouting out bright.

18

'Don't sing them funny songs to the baby or he grow up thinking he is animal. Sing him nice revolutionary songs,' I say standing by door. Tsitsi nearly jump out of she skin with fright. On the bed, baby have been thrashing about trying to crawl towards mother as she sing '*Dangwe rangu*', my firstborn. Now we smile at them and baby start to cry.

All by she own self, she was now singing pure animal sound from the hills, doing that hair-raising yodelling thing called *gule* except there's no *mbira* instrument to accompany she. Something had wake up inside she, me I can tell. She don't even hear us creep inside the house and we find she in she room sitting careless on she bed – one leg point to the mountains and another to the river; no worry or fear on she face. But she is happy to see us. She come back to the house this morning.

'MaiMusindo is away on funeral so I spend one night with Eunice in animal and something,' she say with big happy eyes.

'What animal?'

'Animal something.'

'It's called E . . . Elephant and Castle, Tsitsi.' Shingi solve the puzzle.

Without Aleck around the air inside house feel light. Tsitsi already talk animated like free thing.

'M . . . me I am wo . . . worryful that maybe Aleck is going to tell them police; soon they come and catch us?'

'Aleck only run away from his baby and nothing else,' Tsitsi dismiss Shingi.

We eat *sadza* and them sardines that Tsitsi have buy. All night we talk talk about everything and now we feel like free things while we sit on Tsitsi's bed. We discover by accident that she keep bundle of money hidden inside she mattress but we only laugh about it and talk big things.

And Farayi – no one know where Farayi go and we don't know if he is going to come back. But he have clear everything that was around his bed and take it with him.

We wake up late on Sunday and Tsitsi already in our room putting she baby on us so that baby can pull away the blankets and get us out of bed.

'Why Aleck never make that call to the police to fix us?' I ask Tsitsi and she shrug and pick baby from my chest. I ask the question for the whole week but Tsitsi don't want to let fear stalk she so she don't want to talk about it. She is running the place like it's she place now, and like real mother she is busy making quick and hard decision on everything – food, cooking and the time for eating – and me and Shingi chill. But soon we also have to make hard decision about Tsitsi. If she stay here too long then she and the baby will start eating into our savings and me I will never leave this country. We have to make plan.

Aleck have evil around his waist and evil can chase away other people's luck. How else to explain how you was struggling to hang on to graft except that he chase away people's luck? How else to explain that no sooner have Aleck leave you get new good graft? me I ask. That is after Shingi get brand-new graft at Westminster.

Shingi agree. Last week he come home with this advert for graft that pay £12 per hour. That is more than £2,000 per month even after the tax. Shingi want it and want me to take it too. But it was BBC graft.

Good money, but that's because you will be wiping posh buttocks, it sound like. You want to do something – what is better, to try doing it your own style and risk finding small success, or to do it in undignified pooful way and find big success? I ask him. It's after this that he find Westminster graft and me I cook him big steak on the day he start graft because he is now proper bread-winner. Once Tsitsi go, everything will sail smooth.

Things is getting sweet now because soon me I am cruising at steady 90km/h inside Shingi's pocket. Soon I also cruise at 90km/h inside Sekai's pocket as soon as she come back. That will make total of 180km/h and there's no speed limit in sight. And when I shoo Tsitsi away, soon the big plan come together and me I will be sweet.

The problem with secrets is that sometimes even if you bury them 90km underground they can still come out and chomp your head off, I warn Shingi. He have now start getting streetwise about things; he have grow some small secret: he don't want his family to know that he now work in Parliament because they maybe get wrong ideas and start wanting to dust out his pockets.

I know this native style but I keep his secret safe.

And the weather in London, it now begin to change and put me in good mood as we coast into them unending English summer days. Everything is sweet; them Harare North girls and the flowers mainly. And Tsitsi, now she wake us every morning with baby because now we is buying proper food.

'Tsitsi, you have to be careful with Shingi because his bestest sexy touch is as sophisticate as that of goat.' It's after supper and Shingi give me talking eye.

143

Don't worry, it's only them these good meals make me talk gibberish. These days Tsitsi cook meals that if you don't have strong mind you can only eat while tied down by wire because these meals is so wicked-nice they can make you go raving and talking gibberish all week if you is not careful.

Shingi don't say nothing. Not even one laugh.

She is mother, this Tsitsi. Mothers can cook number-one meals.

Tsitsi take baby to she room because he want to sleep.

Me I don't know why Tsitsi come back to the house instead of going to she aunt. That make two more stomachs now if you count the baby and that will make big dent on your savings, I tell Shingi.

Shingi say nothing.

But she is sweet because now she sometimes leave baby with me so I can bottle-feed him when she is cooking. And the baby now smile at me when I squeeze the milk into his mouth. He like me.

With them days splashing up and down dead on London skyline, Shingi have start to talk like the old comrade that I know. He buy all the food for us and now have heap of money because the week has end and he have been paid again.

Me I am worryful about keeping lot of money inside the house. Why?

Who keep money inside house?

Take it to the bank.

I try to open bank account last week but it's impossible if you is Zimbabwean. Them banks want heaps of papers from you before you can open account. They say it's because of them sanctions that is target at Zimbabwean government people and they relatives. Me I have no time to find all them paper – things from tax office and all.

Then put it inside mattress like Tsitsi, Shingi say. I give him smile. Out of nowhere he do this old-style trick on me. You don't mind keeping eye on my money since you is inside the house most of the time? he say.

Clever idea; get the thief to look after your things and he won't thief them, but I don't say it.

I will think about it because this is the first time I've ever hear of someone trying to turn his friend into his own security guard. Me I don't know whether to feel offended or what, I tell him.

It's because your suitcase is strong and more secure so maybe it's better if I keep the money there.

So now I'm supposed to look after your money?

Shingi look defeated.

OK, for you I'll do it even though I do it with heavy heart, I say after powerful reasoning.

You have not buy me the security guard's cap, uniform and rifle but it's OK, I give him warm grin. If it was anyone else I would not agree big responsibility like this because what happen if the money get thief from me? But you are old friend. It's OK for your money to live inside my suitcase.

Now Shingi sing out-of-tune numbers while taking his showers every evening. He chew up many songs in bad way and step out of the shower with satisfied look on his face and you can tell he is trying to thief his way into Tsitsi's head again.

Me I don't want to disturb you now if you want to catch Tsitsi, I tell him. You are Governor of the Reserve Bank of our house now, so we have to make sure we put this rural fish, flipping and flopping, inside your claws.

One month splash up splash down and dead and there's still no sign of Sekai, Aleck or police. Shingi say he want to take over Aleck's room because it's near Tsitsi's.

It's good move to take position inside Aleck's room, I tell him.

Tsitsi have to go back to she aunt soon otherwise we don't make savings in this house with all these stomachs. I can see it the way the money inside my suitcase is going down because of baby food. If Shingi get his claws on she, then she is going to want to live with us for ever. But me I don't let this disturb my focus.

I start putting them notes down into my likkle diary and try to keep the comrade cheerful.

I am thinking that maybe soon we meet someone that know how to write books, we give them the diary and ask them to write story about me, you and Tsitsi, I massage Shingi ego. My big wish is that maybe when we have find good pen driver he can write cat-and-mouse adventure story about us, make us heaps of money, and maybe for just one night before I fly back home, we can afford chance to stick our noses in at one of them cocktail bars in the city and hit them jugfuls of 'pink pussy' cocktails like everyone is doing. And maybe if the book really sell like them hot cakes, maybe we end up rubbing them noses with the mighty people in London, hitting fattened duck liver and all and going kak kak kak inside them gents' toilets because they say original native laugh can frighten important people sometimes so you don't do it at dinner table. Then me, when I go back home, I have money to buy dozen cattle and invite the whole district to Mother's *umbuyiso* ceremony.

Shingi and Tsitsi pay attention.

After shovelling lots of words around and all over my diary, me I think there is chance that we can hit big fame. I can't guarantee nothing. But we don't want things to catch us by surprise, I put more sugar in Shingi. We have to acquire what they call culture, so we don't get embarrassed in company of proper people.

I stir the sugar inside Shingi and Tsitsi for days and tell them that to learn this culture they also have to ease down some of they native behaviours so they don't frighten them important English people.

It is important to use your eyes, your ears and mouth if you is wanting to catch culture, I teach them. Look, listen and taste. Listen to the music that them people here is listening to, and be careful about them names of the bands that you is listening to. I also write all this in my diary because last week, after we have spend long time reasoning about learning culture, we have hear about them Red Hot Chili Peppers playing at the Brixton Academy. Shingi have big ginger for learning and decide that we go to Brixton Market so he can buy some of they music so we can put it on iPod when he finally buy it. Before I know it dust is rising off them pavements as he start big stand-off with music vendor who keep saying that the band that Shingi is talking about don't exist. That's because Shingi have been asking for the Red Hot Piri-Piris instead of Red Hot Chili Peppers.

That kind of style we have to put inside bin, I tell Shingi. It important to pay big attention to some of them subtly things. I know how these things work. Also keep the native way down in the hole because if he jump out he can cause disorder and then no mother is safe in all of Harare North. 'Don't say, to them English people, "How can I get to Animal Something?"' when you want to say, "How can I get to Elephant Castle?" Enough of that even if you are mother', me I tell Tsitsi. 'Otherwise, we send you back home.'

We talk heaps about how we now have to start getting familiar with them clothes labels if we want to acquire proper culture. All them names like Tommy, Diesel, Levi, iPod, Klein and all them such kind of people that stick they names on people's clothes.

'These is big important people but don't worry too much trying to know who they is because no one know them. Even Tony Blair don't know who Tommy, iPod or Klein is; and the prime minister know buckets of people.' I get ready to finish my lecture and Tsitsi go kak kak kak kak.

'But Tommy and Klein know everyone. That's how big they is. Maybe one day Shingi become real big Governor of the Reserve Bank and also get the right to stick "Shingi" on people jeans. Even on them mothers' knickers. All of them. Then you know we have hit them big times when that happen.'

Tsitsi look at me funny now. Me I ignore she and continue talking.

'Has Uncle Rasputin now drop us some of his money because he is getting away with murder?' I say when Sekai open the front door. She is back. 'If we was back home he will not have been make to pay many herd of cattle for sharp knife like you, but many herd of elephants and rhinos. With all they tusks and horns still there.'

Sekai is not in mood for jokes. She walk straight to the lounge.

'How was the funeral?' I follow behind she. She don't talk but just curl up at the end of couch. She is snorting and wiping tears from she face with tissue paper.

'You . . . you . . .' She shoulders start shaking, she voice crack and she start to cry. Me I don't know what to do with this. I have not even catch what she want to say.

She wipe she face again and stop being porridge. She go quiet.

'I know why you are here and you think that I'm your thing now,' she start without warning. Then she start throwing this other fishwife kind of mouth all over like she don't care, throwing arms in the air and all: Yes I do it with Yakov and the dog witness it. What's the big deal, have you not hear of people having sex?

148

And anyway, this *mbutu* is mine, I can do whatever I want with it. Have I ever ask your cousin what kind of holes he stick his *mboro*?

I have never hear she talk like this. She wipe the snot and catch she breath. 'Now you know everything. Go on and tell your cousin and get this over and done with.'

Then she break down and start crying. 'I was thinking that maybe Yakov would free me from the pain I feel after your cousin cheat on me. Yeee but now it only leave me feeling worse and bitter I end up having quarrel with my brother and telling him that I don't care about his Aids and he can jump off his balcony if he want. And he go and jump. From eighth floor. Now . . .'

Me I don't know what to do with this kind of thing.

'Don't worry. I know what you is feeling; I have feel it too. I forget to visit Mother's grave for two years –'

'You don't know what you talk about,' she sniffle. 'Stop pretending you know everything; you have no idea how I feel.' She even start shouting now. 'And stop hiding behind the memory of your mother so you don't have to face up to your real crimes back home. Do you even know what is happening right now at your mother's village? Do you want me to tell you?' Now she is going out of topic; I get up and get out of the house before she get out of control, this woman.

She is silly woman. I puff my cigarette as I step to the station. She is stupid woman – she want me to do she dirty work. And Tsitsi, this baby food is making big hole in our budget. Women, they always complicate everything.

In the evening I get text message from Original Sufferhead – him that was swinging like crazy on the door of the jackal the day they recruit me. He is now in Harare South – Johannesburg; that's

149

where he run away to when I run away to Harare North and now he is planning to sneak back home because his sister dead. Me I have no ginger for this right now. If the police catch him, then he is not clever.

Shingi say he have see another BBC graft advert – £13 per hour. I give him one look and he know.

Th . . . this p . . . principled . . . m . . . man style will stop you getting back home. But anyway I don't understand why y . . . you w . . . want to go back to Zim if y . . . your mother's village is going to be t . . . take over?' Shingi say. Me I have nothing to say.

19

You can throw baby in the air and catch it with the point of bayonet. That's what they used to do in Cambodia, I tell Tsitsi and she go cold and quiet. Me I'm just joking, Tsitsi. Don't lose sense of humour so fast, me I try to sweet she.

Shingi have been taking position in Aleck's room for two weeks now.

Buy Tsitsi some sweet thing that will make she bite the bait, I advise him. Something like one of them pointy shoes that make London girls go crazy. But Shingi decide to buy denim miniskirt for Tsitsi and one fetching hat for himself.

When he give the skirt to Tsitsi she laugh, 'I'm not prostitute.'

'But every girl in London we . . . wear this.'

'Maybe I ask MaiMusindo,' she threaten and run to she room leaving the skirt on kitchen table.

That is empty threat, I tell Shingi. She have now stop going to MaiMusindo on account she like it here without Aleck.

Shingi look at me and say nothing.

Don't worry, be happy; is it OK if I use some of your money to buy us box of cigarettes and beer to celebrate life? I ask.

Them days jump up and down and dead; miniskirt is still on the kitchen table. Now there's tea stain on it already and Shingi have go out of the house.

'You was right,' I tell Tsitsi. 'No mother can ever wear that.'

Tsitsi look at me with big confusion.

Because now there is no use for the skirt and our floor mop's head is worn out, I take the duct tape that Shingi pick from skip long time ago and I tie the skirt to mop stick. Now we don't have to buy new mop; I have save us £5.99.

Original Sufferhead have sneak back home. He have send another text message and is excite – yari yari yari Comrade Mhiripiri leave the Green Bombers.

You is years behind things, Original Sufferhead, you didn't know this? Tom tell me this before I even run away. Ask me if you want to know, I reply him.

That is big-risk style especially if you is someone that have big stammer. Only someone with smooth-talking style is able to whip any girl with them lyrics, I warn Shingi. He have make another plan to catch Tsitsi. He think he can whip she with them big lyrics, get she head out of gear and before she know it, he will thief his way into she knickers. But he don't want to listen to me.

Lyrics don't work on mother, I warn him again and he still ignore me. Soon he step out of the house because he don't like what I'm saying.

Me I drop £50 on Tsitsi. 'You can use it to go to your aunt if you want. Don't trust Shingi these days.'

Tsitsi now behave like silly hen, she take the money with stupid smile, give me the baby's milk bottle and leave baby with me so she can go shopping for baby things.

In the evening, Shingi step back inside the house and pounce on Tsitsi in the kitchen. He start chewing them words in way that is not grand.

'I b-b-buy youuu sweet music CD soon,' he throw lyric at she.

'No, I don't want music. I have to buy baby nappies first.'
There is short silence now because this have put Shingi's head out of gear. Then he find his way out of it and break out laughing

like this is joke and singing, 'Tsitsi, you are my sweet sweet sugar pie.' Tsitsi think he is joking; Shingi mean it.

'You should only be uncle to the baby,' she laugh.

'OK, I will also b . . . be uncle.'

'You will only be uncle.'

'D . . . do you wa . . . want F . . . Fanta?'

'I want water.'

Shingi talk.

Tsitsi quiet.

Shingi go dump himself on his bed like hopeless man. Later me I go inside my suitcase and drop Tsitsi another £50. 'I told you Shingi is not person to be trusted these days. This is your last chance.'

Shingi is looking troubled that he is only uncle.

But everything going to come together if you keep your eye on the ball, I try to give him more ginger. Biggest weakness is that you don't know how to put girl in tight corner, I teach him now. You and everyone was treating me funny because I was Green Bomber, but boys of the jackal breed know how to talk to people and convince them about anything. If I was you, I would have win long time ago.

Making people think like you want them to think is one of them things that you get teach first as Green Bomber. Don't make no pointless talk. Sometimes you ask question and you only ask simple question because if you ask long questions you also get your head out of gear. Yes or No? that's the style. Once you learn them tricks of Yes or No you can do things. Before someone know it you have put them in tight corner. You can do that with anyone or anything. Even with them girls. People that don't want to answer Yes or No is always suspect, I teach the comrade.

Shingi is quiet.

Is it OK if I use some of our money to buy box of cigarettes?

Shingi is still quiet.

I know this because I see it straight in Goromonzi when we take traitor out to them trees. Girls is easier; "Yes or No" here and there and soon you have put she inside matchbox and she is all yours to put inside your pocket. But you have to have training for these things, I warn him.

'Me I'm worryful about Shingi. He is having diarrhoea and sometimes that can be sign of that big disease with small name. I'm also worryful for the baby; he is my only likkle brother, you know,' I warn Tsitsi but she just look at me funny. 'Shingi have been in prison before, do you know? Anyone who go to prison come out with HIV.'

Love is like termite, I tell Shingi when he come back. He is still desperate and suffer big torment. He is just being porridge.

He wreck himself on beer that night and Tsitsi and me is now worried for him. This frighten Tsitsi now, she even sleep downstairs because she don't trust Shingi sleeping inside Aleck's room next to she room. Me I give the baby goodnight kiss.

That was not bad move, me I tell Shingi in the morning. But improvement is needed. If you give she big fright then you have chance to sniff she front bum. But take it easy, don't lose control too fast.

Shingi say nothing.

Go get good box of shiny condoms or something for she, I advise. But Shingi don't look me straight, you know, like I am try to trick him or what.

Now our Member of Parliament have been paid again. I give Shingi big brotherly smile when the week end; he have get his wages again at his Westminster graft. From now on we call you our MP, I stir the sugar inside him.

Shingi give me them few forced native kind of grins and one big look like he accuse me of things.

You can buy box of condoms this time and sexy underwear.

Shingi say he only want to go out for walk. But he only go and sit under chestnut tree and come back with some tramp that I have see when I see the MFH under the chestnut tree. I remember him because he is gap-toothed, have big wart on his nose and look like he have sleep inside holes for years. He is hop-hopping around on his crutches like injured city fox frightening Tsitsi's baby so it cry.

'Shingi is just trying to bring disorder into the house now because he can't catch you,' I whisper to Tsitsi in the kitchen. 'I have see this *matshayinyoka* before.'

'What is *matshayinyoka*?'

'*Matshayinyoka* – the snake killer – is the person that them neighbourhood's housewives call to deal with snake that come out of its hole to threaten lives of people's children. He is loud, he talk with his hands, and because he is the only man that is around during the day, he is there to kill them snakes for free. For this, housewives allow him to be they substitute husband until the snake have dead. But the snake never die until promise of plate of *sadza* and *nyama* have been made loud and clear.'

Looking at Shingi and Dave the tramp for first time talk talk inside the house is like watching long-lost friends who have stumble upon each each in faraway land where they is not expecting to see each each. Even when them communication difficulties that is caused by language and culture difference is easy to see, they make up for this by hints, winking of eyes, big nods, communist-dictator kind of hand movement and funny out-of-this-world sounds that escape from they mouths in moments of excite.

*   *   *

Maybe it is good idea if we all go play in the park, I say to Shingi on Sunday. That's because when Dave finally leave, yesterday, Shingi look like he have catch the big cheer and this state is still going on. Now the morning promise sunny day and the sky is blue, like it is on one of them English summers that make them days long like stupidity and it feels like everything going to last for ever. Shingi have heap of ginger for this park idea; now he even run to Woolworths to buy some £2 football so we can kick around in the park and be happy like other people.

We is proper London family now, me I give him big smile when he come back with the ball.

There is total of £1,745.13 in my suitcase now if you include my own savings. That is US$3,403.00 with the exchange rate at 1.95. If Tsitsi was not here maybe it would be £2,500 inside suitcase. Or £4,000 is Sekai was behaving proper.

While we is looking for small corner where we can also squeeze and fool around, Shingi is already blasting the ball high up in the air.

Shingi, be careful.

He have now blast the ball into the middle of group of people playing football and disturb they game; they don't say nothing but one of them kick the ball back with crooked touch because it go ten miles from us.

The park is full of people lying on grass frying they bodies in the sun, playing with they kites, playing football and all.

When we find our corner, me and Shingi is fooling around kicking ball to each each because Tsitsi say she just want to sit down on grass with baby and watch. I show Shingi my football skills because he is rubbish. I try to show him the one-two so Tsitsi can see. I try to dink the ball over him. I do the back-heel and hit him one clean nutmeg.

Tsitsi now leave likkle brother on the grass because he fall asleep.

'I play you now,' she say with giggle.

She run around chasing the ball as me and Shingi pass it between us. Then Shingi make mistake and she get it. She kick it far away into distance and it nearly hit this woman that is pushing pram. Tsitsi gasp and giggle with both hand over she mouth and the woman give us looks.

'You can kick better than Shingi because you have real proper control of leg like you are not mother,' I whisper to she.

Tsitsi run and get the ball and pass it to me and now Shingi is the one that have to do the chasing as me and Tsitsi pass the ball to each each. He come running to me but he have the turning range of Routemaster bus so me I turn him this way and that way, that way and this way, inside out, and when it look like he is about to put his back out, I finish him off with one sweet sweet nutmeg.

'Danger; don't mess with me!' I shout and hold my hands in the air so Tsitsi can see. There's heaps of vex on Shingi's face because I'm embarrassing him in front of Tsitsi. He turn around now and chase after Tsitsi. As Tsitsi run for the ball me I see now there's disaster on she bum: it look like she have been sitting on head of goat that has just been cut off – blood on she dress. She have hit the moon, I know straight away. She pass the ball to me but I have to stop the play.

'You have hit the moon,' I tell she and she look at me like she is going to cry in front of us. She don't even try looking behind she dress.

'What should I do?' she ask. Shingi stand miles away shrugging his shoulders. People is already looking at us.

'We go home?'

Me I don't know whether to say yes or no. There's big silence and Shingi not saying nothing even if he is the one that should be helping she.

Tsitsi walk over to the baby and take baby's shawl and wrap

157

around she waist to hide the blood. Baby wake up and start crying. Tsitsi pick up she baby wanting to go and look at us. 'You not coming?'

'People going to look at us funny,' Shingi say.

Tsitsi click she tongue and start: 'You is just like schoolboy that go writing "Shingi was here" inside toilets,' she bite off Shingi's head straight and square.

'What?' Shingi now puff up. But Tsitsi is in vex mood now. She start to dump heaps on the comrade, you know in that style like yari yari yari you still not know that girls go on the moon and you think these English people also don't know; yeee they know more than you and don't look at it funny!

She is almost shouting in the end and me I go kak kak kak because Shingi is looking stunned. 'Me; me I don't know nothing,' I try to crack joke.

'And that's the first truth that ever fall out of your mouth,' she click she tongue with pure rural vex.

20

Tom have also run away from them Green Bombers and is soon supposed to land in UK, *soon you hear from him*. That's Original Sufferhead sending more messages. *Yari yari yari Comrade Mhiripiri run away there too; the jackals is scattered; the movement have lose its way. Yeee and people say the UK government is now investigating Comrade Mhiripiri for crimes against humans; and have you hear about your mother's village? Yari yari yari the* Daily News *want to interview me. Oh, Zim no longer exist.*

Me I have no time for jazz numbers; Original Sufferhead only know fourth-hand stories. *Some memories is not meant to be pissed on any tree just because you can,* I answer him.

Don't open the front door without asking who is outside if there is a knock, do you hear? Tsitsi also have to leave, I tell Shingi and Tsitsi. Tsitsi give me the eye. And Shingi is not paying attention. Just because he have walk Tsitsi back home after park disaster, Tsitsi have been giving him sweet smiles which is very silly and dangerous. And now Shingi think this is the time to catch it; he can sniff sniff front bum right under his nose.

You have to do a TKO move very fast and furious or else she jump out of your clutches now, I coach him. Catch the termite by the head.

He start hitting on she with more fire now. Before I know it he have pull Green Bomber move and start pushing Tsitsi to answer Yes or No if he can visit she room at night.

Keep the pressure on; I become cheerleader now.

Every evening Shingi is now whipping she with Yes or No and she have nowhere to turn. Then it happen one evening – suddenly she get vex and storm out of the kitchen. I go out and buy beer so we can celebrate being one big family.

'I keep warning you about Shingi but you don't listen,' I tell Tsitsi when I come back. 'Why you want to live in this pigsty place me I don't know.'

'You don't want me here?'

'No no no. I am just worryful for likkle baby brother. You can stay if you want.'

Shingi feel like big reject and have run miles inside his head. Now he don't want to talk to Tsitsi no more. He spend time inside his room smoking skunk. I go inside to tell him not to worry because soon he is going to catch it.

Shingi look at me like I make fun of him and don't talk. He look funny because now he start to walk like boy of the jackal breed – all that bold and reckless kind of step; you can tell he have bit of the jackal inside him now after learning to do the Yes or No skill.

If you want to catch girl, you have to make she jealous and then she come running to you like animal. I have sweet plan for you.

Shingi don't believe me but me I'm not worryful; now I want to surprise him with another plan.

There is them those kind of women that is always pushing big camel's hoof that you can see from Scotland – that's the one I drag into the house. All the time I am trying to stop myself from going kak kak kak. She is prostitute, and me I hold she hand just to show off to Tsitsi the kind of wild things that is now coming inside this house that she don't want to leave. She go and hide in she room quick.

Shingi have big foolish grin. He think the woman is English girl, but she is Polish; she can't speak one lick of English. He wonder how I manage to talk to she, I can tell.

I lure she into the squat after I pounce on she on Josephine Avenue. She was busy doing she make-up in front of rear-view mirror of abandoned car when I spot she. Then I spin she some number about how your bed is lice-infested and ask if she want to help you kill them by rolling many times on the bed and crush them likkle things.

Shingi go kak kak kak kak now because his head is full of skunk smoke.

Polish girl is quiet as mouse and look frightened, only giving them East European hard-set looks. But at killing lice, it turn out she is right old riot. Within minutes of them getting into Shingi's room we hear the original native squeal as they task come to sweet end.

Hooray; viva, comrade! I shout loud for Shingi so Tsitsi can hear.

God make man, French fries make round faces, but Shingi and me, we make porridge and number-one steak. But we also make Polish girls cry. That is how I start new diary page that night and show it to the comrade. And when me and Shingi joke with Tsitsi that Polish girl have take all the money that live inside mattresses in this house, the speed and racket that she make on floorboards as she run to she room to see if money is still there is like she have ten legs.

I call Sekai on she mobile phone to check if there is change of mind but she don't answer.

Shingi is in big happy mood because he have finally taste this sweet thing that even Adam and Eve thief from Garden of Eden. Now he leave the door of the house whistling whenever he go to graft. But Tsitsi won't go.

Then Dave the tramp come in with some strange woman, complete with rough face, smoker's throat, rasping laughter, them nose rings, dog and mouse, pockets full of them things and cigarette butts. She hair – it's like some small bird will fly out any time.

'Me I like the direction our life is taking. Soon our squat turn into haunt of them bare bellies and people that pierce everything on they body,' I tell Tsitsi; she is all alone in the kitchen wiping sink for no reason.

In less than half-hour of meeting the woman that Dave have bring, Shingi and I have learn that Jenny have see Shingi outside Sainsbury, that she have been taking care of Dave since he fall from some tree, that she is eco-warrior and have even place an ad in *Loot* saying 'ADOPT AN ECO-WARRIOR AUNT', but nobody want to adopt she because 'I am also gothic, you know'. She used to live in Margate, have try doing plumbing course and was good girl that never used to do them drugs. Then one day when she boyfriend have go to work and she is about to go to plumbing class, she think, 'Oh Jenny, this is boring life, isn't it?' then she pack she bag and hitch all the way to Somerset to pick them strawberries. There some art student sweet she and they start disorderful love that end when she realise he is only able to look after his crayons. That's when she new life begin again.

'Centuries ago in China, local gods use to be threatened with demotion and punishment if they failed to obey people's wishes; after failing to stop the rain, the statue of the god Lung-Wong was imprisoned.' Dave teach us new things too.

'Shingi have never hear this kind of thing. Maybe that's why Chairman Mao try to put things straight,' Shingi say with headful of skunk smoke.

'Why do you talk about yourself in the third person?' Jenny ask Shingi. 'It's funny.'

We is getting bored with talking in the house when Dave say that maybe we go to the Aba Shanti gig at the Brixton Leisure Centre in the evening. He know someone who can get us in for free, he say.

Aba Shanti have four speakers, each the size of shipping container. It is through them speakers that the DJs is unleashing the wrath of Jah, pounding on them walls, floor and roof of the building.

'Jah is so vex he want to tear the whole place apart?' me I ask.

Dave say it's iron reggae dub.

Jenny say something about Aba Shanti gig being the only place where people can discard they mental shackles and become free; she is now sitting on the floor in what she call lotus position.

'There's no segregation and no one makes you feel strange here,' Jenny say but Shingi is still high on skunk and jump in before she have finish what she say.

'Once I used to be bad boy,' he say and Jenny ask why he always do that.

'What?'

'You talk out of turn,' she say.

'No.'

'Yes; you have DID. It's funny. It's weird; I know a woman that used to do that. She was suffering from DID.'

'Here.' Dave hand me bokkle of brandy that he have smuggle. And then he start calling everything that he like 'wicked' and it get my head all out of gear. If there's some good tune, 'Wicked.' The taste of brandy, 'Wicked.' You give him cigarette, 'Wicked.' Everything is wicked.

'Stop calling good things wicked because if you come across real wicked thing, then you will find yourself with no word to describe it. Me I know wicked,' I tell him.

When we leave Aba Shanti, Dave and Jenny follow us back to

the squat on account of Jenny have leave she dog and mouse and she want to collect them.

We get there and find front door raving open. Tsitsi have collect all she things and go. Everything. Even the money inside mattress.

21

Tsitsi gone; Shingi come from his graft and lie on his bed like defeated man – shoes still on and the new hat that he buy from Phat Heads pulled over his face.

Dave have spend the night and all day here because when we find Tsitsi have go we get worryful that soon the police or immigration people come to sniff sniff at our door, and Dave say he know how to make them go away because Dave have live in many squats for long time and know about these things. 'The police need warranty to come inside squat,' Dave say.

Tsitsi pack she things and go and so what? That's she style, I tell Shingi. His face is long like stupidity. He is quiet and don't take his hat from his face. What all this big deal is about I don't understand; mothers go and leave you alone. Always. And life is always not fair, everyone know that. It make you fry wire nails.

You have already hit front bum now and that's all that matter. Now we can make better savings; why you behaving like big baby? I ask Shingi.

I cook supper. Dave refuse the *sadza* and stew that I have cook. Shingi only eat likkle and have no ginger for talk.

Dave, with his unending roll-up in his mouth, talk talk while I eat. He is big visionary and master inventor, that's what he say. He need them long periods of quiet reasoning in order to sink into himself and fish out big new ideas. Me I don't say nothing.

Jenny arrive with she dog suckling one of them dummy teats that mothers stick inside they babies' mouths. She been wandering and foraging around Clapham because today she say she don't feel like going into the city to chase them mobile soup kitchens that is run by charity organisations. She want food.

Yari yari yari dogs and cats can be cured by homeopathy, she talk and bite our sausage.

Now she want our skunk.

Next day I make supper and ask Dave and Jenny if they want any. 'I prefer Marks & Spencer's food,' Dave say.

'I'm OK,' say Jenny.

They is trying to see how far they can push they luck with us. Hoping to wangle big juicy Marks & Spencer's meal out of naive foreigners. And they don't want to eat what we eat because they think it's rubbish, I tell Shingi after supper as I take over Tsitsi's room. I don't want to keep sleeping with Dave and Jenny downstairs.

On Monday, we don't offer them no food, except Coke. They don't go. On Tuesday they go out during the day and when they come back we don't offer them nothing, not even water, and we eat supper while Dave give us those eyes that tell you that the owner of this face step off long time ago.

This is not right what we doing, Shingi say on Wednesday morning.

Wait and see, I tell him.

On Thursday morning Jenny get up early and leave because she say she want to go to the Ace of Clubs in Clapham and then later chase them soup kitchens in the city. But Dave don't go. Even when Shingi get ready to leave for work. Me I step out of the house; you don't want to be left alone with him or else he end up wanting to be friends and then stick to you like tick.

On Friday our friendship with Dave have take unexpected turn;

166

he come back from the bins behind Marks & Spencer's hauling them sausages, bacon, tinned corn, buckets of prawn sandwiches that we will eat for days.

'But don't go into those backstreets at night,' Dave warn us.

'Why?'

'They can be completely mental. Full of strange characters.' Dave is now trying to remain inside the house after the soup disaster last night. That was when we arrive at the squat in the evening to find that, out of the blue, he had rustle up some flaming hot soup for us.

This is not good sign, I warn Shingi then.

The soup turn out to be so hot hot but we brave it. Soon the comrade get sick in the toilet. This morning I am about to kick up big storm but Dave say he is sorry the spices that he use he did not get from Marks & Spencer's and is hotter than he expect and that he will replace some of our food that he chuck into the soup. Then he tell us that them bins at the back of Marks & Spencer's is the best there is in town and only few people know that. Lots of good food – cans of baked beans, beer, sausages, expired foodstuffs – can be found there waiting for us.

'But those are mental backstreets at night.'

Because of this Ma . . . Marks & Sp . . . Sp . . . Spencer bins we is now going to save squillions of money, Shingi say. Maybe he can stay.

Yes, but we is not getting his share of electricity and gas from Marks & Spencer bins, I warn him.

Shingi hand me his mobile phone and there is silence from the other end. Only the sound of slow breathing. Then the line go dead. That's the first worryful thing. Tom? Or Comrade Mhiripiri? Me I also don't want to be known now.

'Don't open the front door if you don't know who is knocking,' I warn everyone. The jackals is scattered.

'The doctor from Rwanda has been arrested.' I can hear Dave talk to Shingi. That's the second worryful thing. Me I don't want no one knocking on our door if they is being investigate by British police. Tom say that's what he hear is happening to Comrade Mhiripiri since he came to Harare North.

'What doctor?' Shingi ask.

'The doctor that was involved in the killing of Tutsis in Rwanda; it's in the news.' The police have catch him now. He run away from Rwanda and have been living in Brighton for years, Dave talk talk like he know anything about them these things. Yari yari yari yeee I was involved in campaign to have him arrest some few years ago; yeee I was campaigner for Amnesty International; yeee Amnesty International they campaign for justice all over the world.

I listen to him talk talk until he have tell and retell the Rwanda story to death. He go on and on about how he have friends that know Peter Tatchell, the homosexual that try to do citizen's arrest on Comrade Mugabe. Shingi also get carried away now and for first time ever he now have opinion on Comrade Mugabe – spinning clouds of jazz numbers about how the president encourage corruption because in Zimbabwe ministers can take take anything they want from anyone. He have hear that from me when I tell him about Mother's village but now he talk about it like he is professor.

When Dave go out to buy tobacco me I want to ask Shingi what kind of style this is. In the end I don't say nothing but only offer him cigarette. He just give me funny face because he know me I can read the score.

Shingi have come late from graft that evening and refuse to cook saying that he is not hungry and that he have headache. He also say he now want to keep all his money for himself.

You OK?

Yes.

How come you not hungry?

N . . . nothing.

You eat anything?

No.

Even on your way from graft?

Shingi walk out of kitchen. I don't get the score that make this jazz number necessary. But I am no civilian so I don't panic.

'Why you talking to yourself, DID man?' Jenny ask. She is back in the house and already causing big racket throwing off she boots on them floorboards.

There is small silence. Dave have been quiet all this time because he is busy helping Shingi spend his money now. I give Shingi all his money yesterday because I want him to feel the truth; if the truth start crawling on his face then he get ashamed, apologise and let me keep it. That was my plan. But he take the money and walk away without shame. Not even thanking me for keeping it. Now they have start to waste it.

'You have to try this,' Jenny break the silence.

'What is it?'

'Smack.' Dave now start to tell Shingi that this smack thing going to make him forget Tsitsi. It work like magic, he say.

This smack thing – that's Shingi's money being wasted. I am sitting tight in this house hoping all this don't end with people spinning jazz numbers about my past. I look in the mirror and I see my beard is growing long.

Shingi have start to leave pieces of bread in kitchen cupboard so that he can feed the rat. Jenny has spin him some number about animal rights and why we should learn to live with the rat. It's complete waste of money; none of this will have happen if I was in charge of our money. But I just spend time in my room because these days our house is having big headache I can see.

Last week there was syringe in the lounge. Then there was another in the kitchen. Yesterday one was lying on staircase. Now there is even one inside toilet bowl. And evenings now end with everyone curled up on floor of Shingi's room like they is dead. I grow my beard with skill.

From window of my room I can see miles into Brixton. My window look everywhere; it's one of them sad eyes that look at you when you come to our house. I spend my time sitting by window and look outside at the world while Shingi and his friends slam them doors in the house.

I spend heap of time by the window writing the diary about us, pushing heaps of thoughts around inside my head. I am making big effort to keep big cheer on my face and don't want to sow too much bad ideas about Shingi. But I cancel out the page that I have write about Shingi. I buy another padlock so I can have two on my suitcase because me I don't trust Shingi and his friends no more. Maybe soon they try to go through my suitcase. I don't even recognise this Shingi. And when I find that he also now keep his suitcase locked all the time, I have to try hard to stop myself from finding out if his toothbrush in the bathroom can also work good as toilet brush.

22

Dave slam the front door so hard again and again, our house nearly fall down. He have been cheat while buying drugs. He think that he is buying crack but it turn out to be something for making dogs do heaps of poo.

Jenny do this violent brain-rattling laugh that shake even the doors and windows of our house. She dog even start to bark.

In the evening there's heaps of vodka bokkles going around and everyone in Shingi's room sound loud and pathetic. By midnight Dave is lying on floor like dead, Shingi have pass out on his bed and Jenny is lying in pool of vomit in bathroom.

On Monday Shingi forget to go to work. In his room things is quiet. I sit on my suitcase by window most of the day, polishing my screwdriver.

I go out wandering in Brixton Market and I bump into old Tim buying fish. He is with the knife that he always talk about in his shop. He give me big funny grin when he see me but I shake his hand to make clear that I don't do no hard feelings.

'Hi, Shingi, this is my wife Diana.'

His knife is one of them big mamas that look like they wear apron all the time when inside house and always smell of flour and baking powder. Tim is looking worryful as he introduce me to she.

She have warm smile and we try to make small talk as Tim turn around to haggle with fishmonger. I ask she if Tim allow she to hold TV remote control at home, and she go kak kak kak and I don't know what's so funny.

Tim join us; he look vex and complain about how the fishmonger try to use them ways and habits that is normally used to put down them poor folk. I nod as his knife watch because Tim is talking straight to me saying he also come from poor background. He continue with this outpouring so that there's no chance of us talking about how I leave his graft.

'Oh people are sometimes not treated fair,' he cry and me I agree until he try to tell me that in England another way them poor folk used to be put down was by being ridicule for being not good at holding they fork and knife.

'Now, me I don't agree. Even if I'm not English, there is some things that I know first hand. I have see Dave's use of fork and knife, which cannot be classify as five-star skill.'

'Who's Dave?'

'Some homeless bum. One day we go to Elser Cafe. There Dave demonstrate his fork-and-knife skill in grand way. While he is busy doing battle with piece of meat, it shoot off his plate like missile, fly into the air, out through the cafe entrance and it land somewhere in Israel. That's the kind of accident that don't happen with someone who have got good fork-and-knife skill.'

Now this pathetic drunk smackhead appear out of nowhere, and out of the three of us, he come straight to me to ask for spare change.

'Spare some change, brother?' he say, shaking and giving me this long coalface; his eyes drop as he try the old emotional blackmail style. He press so many buttons on me I want to close them my eyes so tight you can't swipe razor blade through my eyelids.

'People. They should know when and when not to bother other people. I don't like saying no because, deep down, I am nice man. I even have them friends who is like you. But right now I have

172

to tell you the truth straight and square: don't ever talk to me like that; you don't know me.'

He drop his eyes, throw curse and walk away.

'Just because me I'm black native and he's black don't give him the right to pick me out of all them people. Sometimes you have to take firm stand with them things otherwise you get run over,' I tell Tim and his knife. They is struggling to smile because they give me them tight grins like they don't want to be involved in this kind of thing.

I go to Internet cafe to check my email and there is email from Tom. He have really now land in the country and is asking if he can come visit me and *have you see Comrade Mhiripiri? People say he is after you because when the police start chasing him back home he had use some of his money to pay only part of bribe to cover up for you but you let him down. They say he is bitter man now.*

I get up and leave.

I pick one copy of the *Metro* newspaper from the station and go back to our house.

At home I find Jenny and Dave all worryful and tense. They say someone come here looking for me while I was out. When they tell him I'm not here he say he will wait and he spend hours sitting alone in the kitchen. Then he leave without saying one word.

'Did he say he is looking for me, you sure?'

'Yes.'

'Don't open front door if you don't know who is knocking.'

I sit on my suitcase and read the *Metro* paper from front to end. I don't want to think about how much money Shingi have got left now.

The news have not change since I last read the *Metro*; stories about Israel and Palestine, Iraq and another story about Tony

Blair and how his Christian beliefs not good for his graft. The only interesting thing inside is in column where they is talking about the Ancient & Honourable Society of Rat Catchers, some organisation with members who is quality professional people. The society have big reputation, with each member average about 600 rats per year, all catched on farms in Sussex and Berkshire where the honourable society organise weekend visits for members. Membership is £550. That is more than what Shingi have got left now.

I also read about how long time ago in England men who was dying and don't want to turn into some sorry and poor sight would just go to edge of cliff and jump off. And if they don't have the strength to make journey to cliff then there was always this club called 'the holy maul' that was keep at the back of the local parish for any family that need it. The family take it and go maul the man. I wonder if Shingi brave enough to face the holy maul if something happen that leave him too weak to go jump off cliff in Dover.

Out on our road some racket break out involving woman with big temper. I go out to check what this is all about. It's Jenny. Dave and she is all on they way back and she clash with neighbour who live two doors from us. The *jambanja* start when Jenny's dog drop *kaka* on the pavement right in front of our neighbour's gate and she don't bother to pick it. Then this old man come out of house and come down on she like big swan, asking she if she is going to pick that up. But Jenny is used to this kind of thing; she just start throwing she mouth in rough way: yeee children is dying of starvation in Zimbabwe and you come out whinging about dog shit in front of your house; yeee let's get perspective here please!

The whole thing descend into one roof-shaking shouting match about 'you people' and neighbours stick they heads out of

174

windows; I get worryful because I don't want wrong attention being attract to us. I thief back into the house and don't want anything to do with this. I don't want police to come sniff sniff around our house.

You and your friends now getting careless about things, I say to Shingi when they come inside. Just because you have your papers OK and don't fear police, don't have to be selfish about things.

He just sit on his bed and start rolling skunk. He have forget to go to graft today.

I write to your mother and tell she what's going on, I warn him. I will write letter and say Shingi is working in Parliament and earning tons of money. Why you hide it from your family that you have Parliament job now? Back home inflation have go crazy at zillion per cent, your family is starving and you is wasting money on drugs here.

'Shingi! You OK?' It's Jenny, but there's no answer from Shingi.

Jenny start asking if he have headache again. Dave think Shingi is having whitey because he smoke too much skunk.

'But he's talking to himself,' Jenny tell Dave. They don't know what Shingi is saying.

'He's talking in tongues,' Dave laugh.

Our house is full of skunk smoke. The next thing that I hear is this hoarse and gnarled primitive howl that sound like it is being tear off Shingi's throat.

Jenny's dog start barking and Jenny start giggling with fright. Now Shingi is doing deep belch, making animal grunts, breathing deep and loud and groaning. I know this number; he is just pretending he is possessed by vex spirit.

'He's getting the shakes,' Dave panic.

Shingi is only trying to frighten me because I have give him tongue-whipping and threaten to write to his family and tell on him. I know this kind of style. Shingi have do it before back home. Even Uncle Nhamo used to do it.

I sit tight waiting to hear if Shingi is going to say something about my past. But he start calling out for his mother. Dave and Jenny is out of they depth now. This racket go on for hours and when it die down, the first thing I hear clear is Jenny. 'I'm hungry,' she say. She want to go check if there's anything in them bins.

'No way, this time of the night?' Dave don't want to go. 'Those backstreets get completely mental at night.' He make big moan; yari yari you get stabbed by weird people for no reason; yari yari I don't want to deal with mental people.

I lie on my bed listening and wearing my past like it is some very tight gown; I don't want no one tugging at it.

I get up and go to toilet and as soon as I sit suddenly there's loud rude knock on the front door. On the toilet I sit straight up. I hear Dave run to the door. He don't even ask who is outside and just fling the door open like idiot.

It's them the police. They is following on complaint that was make by neighbour on account of the quarrel and all the racket that Jenny's caused.

Jenny come down to join Dave at the front door and they is busy talking to the police now. They talk and talk for some time and I don't know what they say but they make them go away.

23

Shingi stop going to work altogether; I know that in Parliament this kind of behaviour is what can get bosses vex; miss graft two three times and you is out straight and square.

I call Sekai on the phone and she send big earthquake down the wire and it rumble inside my head. She have slip back into she nasty self now.

'Now stop childish games. I know things about you but I am not blackmailing you and threatening to climb St Paul's dome to shout it to the world.'

Then she go on yari yari yari, yeee I am not trying to shame you but doing you big favour because you have to face up to your life like all of us. 'And did you hear that General Nguruve has send your Green Bomber friends and the army to your mother's village and now everyone has been moved away?' she say.

Some kind of animals breathe and scatter your thoughts like heap of leafs; I spend all day in bed trying to collect my head into one heap. First you is at the mercy of them winds – gust sweep it in one direction, another blast in another direction. Then this thing scatter it all over. Still you try to keep them things together.

The wind blow into our house and into my room; it scatter and gather papers and things into heap at the corner of room. I sit on my suitcase by window doing nothing.

There is big rough knock on the door and I run downstairs to ask who is there but there is no answer from outside. I ask again who is there but I only hear them heavy footsteps walking away.

I run upstairs to my room to look outside from the window but on the street there is only two kids playing with they bikes. I go back to polish my screwdriver now. I polish the thing until it shine like trumpet. The only fault with screwdriver is this small lump and dimple near the tip which I am suspecting was caused by Paul testing car battery and maybe some spark jump onto the screwdriver and melt it. The lump look like the wart that Dave have on his nose. Now I polish the wart so it twinkle like likkle star. This house need order.

In the kitchen, Shingi stagger and talk like he have drink too much. His left hand is twitching in funny way and his mouth is hanging. On his mobile phone there is two text messages for me from Original Sufferhead: all that US$4,000 was just big jazz number, that's what he say. *Cde Mhiripiri just wanting to hit people's pockets to make himself rich. He try it on many people. Angirayi was also running around because Cde M say they want US$4,000 from him. Angirayi never find the money and he is still there and police not even interested in him or any of us because what they want is Cde M because he have humiliate them many times and Goromonzi police inspector have got scores to settle with him. And now people say he is part-time BBC in London.*

The rush of whirlwind inside my head scatter me all over. Mother, she lie heavy in my heart. The head swirl. The air inside our house turn and shift my head into sixth gear. From way beyond the blue hills inside my skull, back in my rural home, where Mother's bones lie scattered, trampled and broken by JCB, where my grandmother used to go to the river to carry the water, come back and keep the fire burning, I now hear them voices tell me that I am still among the living.

I put the screwdriver in my pocket, and manage to leave the house without running.

It's not right.

I march straight to the chestnut tree. Among them all the homeless and asylum seeker, there he is, wearing his brown cap. Before I even speak he give me one tricky look. I look down at my feet, but he hit me square in the face.

'Speak, young man,' say the Master of Foxhounds.

I clear my throat but nothing else come out.

'Have cigarette.' He flick the cigarette box open and stretch his hand out in my direction. Sitting some few steps from him, I have to decide whether to stand up and walk to him or wait and see if he come to me. For funny reason I stand up, reasoning that maybe he meet me halfway. He remain seated.

The moment I step across the halfway line onto his side, it is like he have cast some spell. Before I can reach for the cigarette, his eye jump jump inside its socket and give me this look that fix me to the spot. I don't know whether to turn back and sit down or to take his cigarette, but my hand, on its own, shoot out. He pull his hand in slight and draw me in. I stretch, reach out and manage to pull out one cigarette from his box. It is time to return to the spot where I have been sitting, which now look like long long journey. I feel light as the wind. I am not sure if giving back his cigarette will help me get upper hand again.

My feeties bolt. They take me down Coldharbour Lane. I get to them traffic lights at the corner of Atlantic Road. I have to go back; I have to face up to him.

He is still there when I get back. I try to catch his eye but he don't want to look and now again pretend he don't know me as usual.

'Why you play cool style and try to deny me? In case you don't see – the past stand tall before us, the wind is blowing she skirt up, and there underneath she, soon I see you huddling down; no more cover for you now,' I hit him square on the face with the question as I light cigarette. He look at me with heap of confusion on his face.

'Do you remember?' I puff out big cloud of cigarette smoke. He don't know what kind of style I'm hitting him with. 'I can get you in trouble with Amnesty International people if you is not careful. Do you remember me? I spend time trying to tell people back home that you being here is just big jazz number. Then I hear the truth. Do you remember this son of the soil?' I ask again and now everyone is paying proper attention. The MFH don't say nothing. I stand close, holding my hands behind to show him what kind of style I can do. My beard point down at his feeties. 'They can walk those feeties but have they ever step on truth? Truth is like snake; you step on it and it bite you straight and square, I know because I have step on it. Now do you remember this son of the soil?'

He is still trying to deny me because we is in front of everyone.

'Goromonzi. That's where I get born again, my friend. On the day the sun forget to shine. Among them tall trees; I blow and trees hide they faces. And you, where was you?'

I change gear. 'You OK there, old man; do you know this kind of style?' I give him the look and I can sniff sniff that he have big fear squatting behind his one eye for the first time.

'You know this kind of style, eh? From them those days? Those days when we go to Goromonzi because of them British-sponsored MDC party supporters. They was crawling on and under every rock, man, even beating up some of our supporters. And you, where was you?'

Now everyone looking at me and the MFH.

'Two dozen boys of the jackal breed, but only one of them carrying the only truth in his back pocket – that was me when we meet outside Goromonzi police station. The son of the soil give few revolutionary barks and we break into song when start to march inside police station: *Zimbabwe yakawuya neropa yakawuya nehondo!* Do you get this style, eh?' I give the MFH side glance to get his head out of gear.

'We sing and wave them sticks in the air and the earth shake on that day. We march through police station gate singing and the sound make you feel like old fire have start to burn inside you. Do you want me to remind you? Now do you want forgiveness, comrade?' I point my beard at the MFH and he give me the slow eye. Oliver get up and go.

'I run you the whole story if you have forget. When we march to charge office and the officer-in-charge is on the veranda watching some of his men playing game of draughts in the warm morning sun, who was the one that shout, "Is it not too soon for your men to be playing draughts when enemies of the state is still leaping all over us in our sleep and clogging them skies?" Officer-in-charge take one look at us and know who we is because we come with heaps of forgiveness; we is them sons of the soil. In England they don't allow me to give forgiveness but tell me if you want forgiveness for everything.'

'Forgiveness for what?' The MFH throw glances at everyone around like he want agreement from people that this is silly thing. 'I don't know what you talk about, young man; forgiveness for what?' He shake his head, stick cigarette inside his mouth and look another direction like he is getting tired of this.

'Wrong question,' I whip him straight and square. 'Ask again, and if you was listening to me you will know what question to ask.'

'Peace peace peace, make love not war,' Peter start shouting this kind of poem.

'Look at history, my friend. The path of many of us is set by few fat bellies with sharp horns and hard hoofs; they gore and trample you the moment they know you see through they cloud of jazz numbers. And you want me to fight them with poem?' I lick Peter straight and square. The MFH blink like goat.

'I remind you the story again. "Where's the traitor? We bring them bags of forgiveness," that was the style. But now your beard is gone; just some old part-time BBC who never reply letters.'

I get into gear and start singing the story now. '"We only have one and he's going to court next week. We can't release him," that's what the officer-in-charge say. Big mistake that, if you remember.' I spin on sole of my boot and look everyone in the eye. I cough and clear my throat, everything scatter like leafs inside my head and now I hear the roar of thousands of pigeons flapping they wings as they take off to the sky. Over Harare North the sky is dark with swarms of pigeons that have been frighten off buildings and squares by my coughing. Thousands of wings flapping above the city and the MFH is wondering what I am looking at. I give him the story again.

'*Zimbabwe yakawuya neropa yakawuya nehondo*, that was the song. Do you remember the song? When we break into it, who launch into this speech: "Who do you think you serve by protecting enemies of the state when the president have make it clear that we should give them all the forgiveness," his beard pointing at the problem in front of us. Time come when every man have to decide which side they is on.

'Officer-in-charge suddenly realise quick that even if we is sons of the soil, we have sharp nose for treason. Them stocks clang open and the traitor is quickly handed over. We drag him away to the forest where it is easy to give him plenty of forgiveness. But that was not the only traitor I deal with on that day and you, you will never know. You only chose money. You, you know nothing. You never know of the other traitor, the shoe doctor inside my head. But that's the one that I take out first. Soon I am hitting him with them Yes or No questions and he is bawling

182

his lungs out because he know he is the first to go. Soon I hit him with the truth. Truth is like granite rock because if someone hit your head with it, your head feel sore. One rock of truth can crack your head, comrade commander. Now, after all this heap of time I step on the truth about what game you play. It bite my foot and I wake up to find that you, you was spinning US$4,000 jazz numbers around my head. Everything that the boys do you have betray. You have become traitor. So what was it all for to you, the struggle?'

'What was it all for?' He laugh and shake his head like this is silly question. Now he start going kak kak kak kak so loud like I am fool; his mouth is wide open like cave, the rotten back teethies is pointing. 'Even today you still have milk coming out of your nose, young man. Zimbabwe was a state of mind, not a country.' He laugh like maniac.

'You want forgiveness or what?'

'Forgiveness forgiveness,' now people is starting to shout and the MFH has big alarm on his face.

'You want forgiveness?'

'Forgiveness, forgiveness!' everyone is shouting now and I'm rolling up my sleeves.

'Forgiveness, forgiveness, forgiveness!' the crowd now sing. The MFH is lugging football-size eye and I'm trying to get to him but already there is thrusting of arms and elbows everywhere as Peter and them other guys is now all over me trying to restrain me. My screwdriver fall out of my pocket onto the ground. The MFH get up, throw his arms up in the air and shuffle away with fearful looks on his face. By the time everyone let go of me the MFH has go down Coldharbour Lane. I pick up my screwdriver and run down the road trying to find him but there's no sign of him.

In the sky, the pigeons have clear out and the sun is falling out of the sky behind big mama cloud and my head slide into sixth gear. My feeties start causing big racket and taking me all the way to Brockwell Park.

I walk into the park and my bladder is full. I want to pee; I go straight to them trees on the edge of the park and don't care if people can see me. The biggest tree. It have one untidy small anthill growing on its foot and the anthill is crawling with them termites. I pee on them straight and square.

I walk from the tree and I come across crippled squirrel trying to drag himself towards bush but he is failing because the back legs look like they was squash by wheel of car or something so he is trying to drag them across. His back is broken; he look pathetic. Soon the thing is going to die; I can't leave him like that.

I take out my screwdriver, put my boot on squirrel's head to pin him down, position my screwdriver right behind the head; on the spine. One quick jerk of the wrist, and snap. The screwdriver go through the neck right onto the grass and wet ground below. The squirrel don't even feel anything. No pain, no movement except them front paws that shiver like the squirrel now go spastic. Blood squirt everywhere. I put him out of his misery and put back some order into his life.

I pick the dead thing and throw him inside bin and wipe screwdriver with my shirt.

My feeties take me around the pond. I sit down. I can't sit. The trees, they is swaying around because of wind. The winds is causing havoc inside our house I know; the windows was open when I leave.

Some old tune have start spinning inside my head; *Togure Masango*. Low volume; it is like listening to faraway people. Even my breathing now feel like it come from some place else; from way beyond the hills. Everything fade away to great distance.

In the sky one big mama cloud is gathering all its children

around sheself. I look at she and she look at me with she big face. My feeties, they take off again. Out of the park. The air hold still, something shift but I am still among the living and I breeze through them Brixton streets like the winds as darkness fall down like dust on Harare North. I can walk. I can't smile. I get hungry. My feeties is vex, my stomach is crying and I am walking into them mental backstreets; I want Marks & Spencer's food.

To the left of Marks & Spencer's bins, some distressed cry for help rip through unlit air. I turn my head to look: there is brain-jangling argument exploding between two people. Shingi is still not sober but sober enough to be frightened. He is step-ping backward and shouting for help. The big tramp in front of him is holding sharp instrument, wearing T-shirt only and pair of dark underpants. Before I can even shout his name Shingi have drop his bag of food and bolt down dark alleyway. I hold my screwdriver tight.

I have not even take dozen steps but I know that the winds have already rip the sky open; two drops of rain have already find my face on them backstreets of Harare North.

I get to the alleyway. There is no sign of anything. I run to the next turn and I see them turning into another backstreet; Shingi is now limping and the tramp's bum jumping in the air like heap of jelly. But he is now chasing the tramp.

'Shingi, Shingi,' I shout. They disappear.

'Shingi,' I call. Above us big mama cloud throw down one of she children – some big bale that come down crashing onto the streets like great water sachet soaking everything. I get glimpse of Shingi ahead and call his name; water run down my face and go inside my mouth. Big mama o' she throw sheself down at them pointy roofs and church spires – they rip through she and she splash into tatters on the streets of Harare North. I see Shingi soaked; his trousers heavy with the blood of big mama, he holds onto them and hobble into shadows of tall buildings. That's the last I see of him.

Poo happens o'! And the world is not fair place. That's the style of this funny place. It make you fry wire nails. Around the corner, on them wet pavements of Harare North, Shingi is one untidy heap. Naked tramp has give him forgiveness and is splashing his feet away into the night, far from long hands. I feel helpless. I am useless. Everything is useless. I don't know what to do.

And the woman at other end of 999 call – she is also useless. I hear it in she voice; she want to ask too many questions – where am I from, who am I and all that stuff but 'sorry you is not going to get that from me. Me I know your style, I know you is going to put this information inside long hands of immigration people and police. Me I don't want to be witness o' no.' Me I hang up.

I don't wait around for ambulance people or police to arrive. I go sit under the chestnut tree where I can see police car and ambulance flashing blue and red inside dark alley and reflecting on them wet tarmac. The policeman talk talk. The ambulance people point they torches and talk heaps too. The rains have stop falling now, the preacher outside KFC have go home, the *djembe* player outside Tube station have pack his things and go, chestnut tree is empty and street pavements only have handful of people pointing they umbrellas to the sky where big mama cloud jump out of.

I light cigarette and watch the ambulance drive slowly down Coldharbour Lane towards King's College Hospital and police go down Brixton Road to police station.

World is not fair place o' and poo happen in it. Before we go to bed that night Shingi is fighting for his life.

'He have been stab stab all over his head and neck in those mental backstreets,' I tell Dave when he come back to our house.

I have just finish washing my clothes in bathroom because they was wet and also have squirrel blood from afternoon.

'Shingi decide to go alone in them mean backstreets because you and Jenny won't stop yari yari yari with them other junkies outside Brixton station and you don't accompany him.'

Now, just because I have tell him what have happen, Dave is pushing them big eyeballs in front of me like he care.

'I'm sorry, we was –'

'I have no time for this.' I step up to my room.

24

You want to go check on your old comrade to see how he is doing and if this is serious injury; two times you go as far as hospital gate; two times you turn back. Then you try the phone.

Late at night, Jenny knock on your door and ask if you want cup of tea. It's the first time she ever do this. She look worryful and sorry for you because you is sitting tight on your suitcase reasoning hard. She have big raft of bogey hanging from she nose. When she come with the tea, the bogey is gone and you don't know where it have drop so you don't drink the tea.

Shingi lie in intensive care in deep sleep. Maybe he is bandaged head and neck with them black and blues all over his face, I don't know. But he will be OK.

The air in our house is stiff and blue. No racket from Dave or Jenny downstairs; I have tell them to keep away from Shingi's room now and stay in downstairs room only. The only sound coming into my room is the here and there rush of cars down the road.

My window look down onto our road. I sit stiff by the window. On the street two foxes is getting into fight. I puff cigarette, breath like ghost and wipe sweat from my big forehead.

And Shingi's mother? *It is my big painful duty to tell you that* . . . I run out of words and don't know what else to write. I put my pen down and reason even if she's not his real mother, but his mother's sister.

Shingi going to be back home one day; he is going to bring

heap of money home; I want them tight lyrics only. No stiffness. If his family ever know this is what have happen things will get funny and Shingi have to explain to everyone how everything happen – he is going to have to tell his family how he nearly lose plot in London, make friends with bums, get into drug and lose graft. That story is not going to fly off Shingi's tongue. What will MaiShingi say?

I go inside his room. His suitcase is locked. I pick it up and fling it against wall once and it burst open; things fly onto the floor. The money too. There's now only £360 of it. I spend whole hour going through papers trying to find his mother's address.

When you is trying to write tight letter, it's like hanging fat dictionary by rope and cracking the old whip on it until them words fall out onto the floor. Them wrong words keep falling out and you have to keep sweeping them away and then whip your head some more until the right word fall out. That's what happen when I start writing to Shingi's mother. In the end me I don't write letter that is too long but I keep it tight and small.

My head go into sixth gear now because me I have to say something to Shingi. You can never know what to say to someone that is fighting for life. What do you say? That's the first question that perch on my head like big bird. I have not see him and I have not say one word to him since that evening. That make me feel heavy. I have to say something today.

I buy Shingi two bananas and two apples but I don't know what to say. So I go lie on my bed and rehearse for when I finally find courage to go into hospital. Maybe he will be asleep and can't hear me. But I have to talk. Say something so the heart stop feeling so heavy; tell him everything is going to be sweet and swanky in the end.

I let them things come out like you do when you is good old

189

friend. Me I will talk about everything. Crack them jokes like we used to do in them good old days.

I will talk about how brave he is. I will tell him about the story that I read when he was still OK; that story in the *Metro* about how English people used to go and jump off some cliff.

If you was fit to walk, I know you would have walk to Dover cliff and make one brave jump and end all this in neat way, I will crack joke.

I have check at the back of St Matthew's Church and the bad news is that there is no holy maul there, I will laugh like we would have do if he was fit. He is old friend Shingi. We is going to go kak kak kak about everything when it have come to pass; things going to be OK, I know. Comrade Mhiripiri have been exposed now; I don't have to find US dollars no more. No more fighting over money and all. I only have to step back home now.

Maybe some fat nurse is going to float in to check all is OK. Maybe I will go quiet until she go out of the room. Then I want to make the comrade feel swell inside if he can hear me. I will talk about them good old times and all. Like the time he start his graft in Parliament and bring home copy of *Private Eye* magazine that some big man forget in the toilet. By the time he get home, the comrade have learn heap of words and already showing off, calling Members of Parliament 'm'learned friends'. But another week have not even pass when he come back moaning about some big battle he have in the gents' toilet with one joist of poo. He swear it can support roof of the House of Commons.

That one was jazz tune that you was spinning me, no? I will joke now. If he try to get his attention to the soft ingredients involved in the making of them m'learned friends' meds then he will know it is impossible for them to make poo that can be put to such powerful use as he suggest.

It has to be one of them your graft mates that secretly dump that log, I will laugh at him. That is if it's not you.

I want to ask him how the hospital people will take him to toilet.

Some of them things coming out of you, I'm sure is going to be like caveman's club, both in shape and size. Maybe now we have find better replacement for holy maul, me I will go kak kak kak to myself. Maybe his finger will move.

What kind of food you want me to bring for you?

Maybe all them fruits that I keep bringing will keep piling up because he don't eat them.

I can bring some steak or porridge if you want? Or roast pheasant with the old goose liver and spiced chutney and all that kind of fancy stuff? I will try every button; with them Parliament people, you never know what kind of tastes grow on them in Parliament. He is still M.P.

I take one of them bananas from the side of my bed and start eating it.

Now I have to talk about how I have already fix him. I have even make photocopies of the letters that I post yesterday. We is going to have good laugh about this when it's over. I have to practise reading the letter.

P D N F – Please Do Not Fold
Dear Mother
    Time and ability plus double capacity have force my
pen to dance automatically on this paper. I hope this letter
find you in good health, if so, doxology.
    Well, everything here is just half lemon half sugar, to
make it Schweppes lemonade. Me I am as healthy as
Harare North dog. You will understand if you come here
and seen how well fed them dogs is.

Me I have good news. My long time here now pay me back. I'm confirm to you that I now work for the House of Commons. It is House of Parliament here. Tell Aunt MaiAngirayi. Me I see important people. Even the prime minister. Maybe now you can say that you is mother of Member of Parliament!

Me I love you spontaneous and as I sit perpendicular to the ground and parallel to the wall I only think of you, since you is good mother even if you are not my real mother. I love you more than my shoes love my feet. I will send pair of top-notch English shoes.

Me I have to pen-off here because I have to cook. Sleep tight and don't let them bedbugs ever bite you. Yours faithfully, your son

Shingi

PS: I will send money next month.

Your room is still full of disorder, I also want to tell him. I pick your passport from floor in your room. I have it for safe-keep. Also the mobile phone. It have been on charger for days because no one disconnect it since you get hit. I remove it from socket and take it for safe-keep too.

I also want to talk about how I bust his suitcase looking for his mother's address but I can't because I have see them heap of letters from his family; some funny stuff. Especially from Shingi's Uncle Sinyoro. He is the one that used to pay Shingi's school fees and other things that MaiShingi can't afford. He is now Senior Officer in Ministry of Education but behave like retired colonel – grumpy and not tolerate different opinion. Shingi have tell me that he is also now divorced Christian and is quiet man living

192

alone like hermit and always speaking polite with strangers, pharmacists behind counter or vegetable vendors. But under them sheets he is brutal bastard who frighten his wife and children, killing cats that eat his biltong.

There's heap of vex letters from Education Officer and it seem like it's because Shingi have write letters calling him stiff-necked believer. So Sinyoro get busy wetting himself with vex throwing rough mouth at Shingi and all that kind of stuff. Some of them letters inside Shingi's suitcase talk funny things like how Shingi's grandmother is concerned that Shingi need to be cleansed of bad spirits. She don't see it that Shingi pretend to be possessed sometimes because that's his style for scaring people.

25

All I need now is £240 then I can buy £500 ticket straight and square. Before the sun is up I will have land back home. Uncle don't deserve his money back since he do nothing about Mother.

I come from graft hunt and bump into Dave as soon as I walk inside the house. I don't want to talk to him. I don't want to kick fuss about him. Even when he spend most of the time lying in room downstairs doing weapons grade farts all day.

'Hi,' we say to each each when our eyes clash. He march to me with big purpose and give me one of his flyers.

Professor of All Psychics, Master Visionary & Inventor
   Do you have problem with: immigration, love, cheating, abuse, relationships, infidelity, stubborn children, health, keeping the one you love happy, finding a job, money? Specialising in cleansing and purification, palm and chakra readings. Call me for results today, tomorrow may be too late! If you want to know your future, Professor has mastered the art of uncovering the negative energy that affects you in everyday life. Try these for a start: 1) Love spell – take one red apple and core it. Write the name of the person you love three times on parchment paper with red ink. Place the parchment paper into the core hole, pour honey into it until full and place the apple near the home, car or job place of the person. If the person that you requested to love you doesn't come to you in two days, CALL ME! 2) Spell for wealth & success – on a green stone write

your name and your three wishes. Wrap the stone up in green paper and keep in the pocket on the left side of your chest. If you fail to see any change in your finances or job in two days, CALL ME!

'I give you one day to go and then no more.'
Dave look at me like I am throwing away help.

I go to my room; I light cigarette; I go to the kitchen again; I look out of window and there's family of them Romanians that live across road. They is looking at me through they window like I am on TV. I drink Coke. I can't sleep, and in the morning the bad news come, give our door one kick and the door burst open; the news stand cackling into our house: this is hopeless case, is what the hospital think about Shingi.

I have not see Shingi yet; maybe hospital people start asking funny questions and end up saying I'm illegal in this country. That's they style.

Maybe Shingi now just like someone that have been whip by stroke – mouth hanging, dribble coming out. I can't eat all day; I go to bed early.

He's back in our house. In wheelchair. He can't talk. I feed him because now he can't even move one finger. I take him to toilet. Again.

Again.

And again.

I wipe the comrade's bottom so many times, shove his body around and wash his soiled pants until this turn into strong argument for banning of food. Even the toilet seat break in half and now there is three pieces of it. But I can't stop feeding him; food is where all problems start.

In them sagging depths of his wheelchair, silent and staring at the ceiling all day, Shingi and his scraggy beard fill up the whole house. I have clean him up now; I try my best.

In the morning I get up and make porridge. Dave is still around even when I have give him warning.

'You need life skills to budget your money now if you have no job,' he say while I'm busting my head trying to figure out what to do about Shingi. He go on yari yari yari I have got life skills; yeee I can do my sums right when I get paid social benefit and make sure things balance.

I eat my porridge and say nothing.

26

I don't buy bananas for Shingi because he won't eat them now I know. I eat all those that have pile up in my room. All of them.

Shingi's mobile phone start ringing and it's them his London relatives' number flashing on the screen. I ignore it; I don't know what to tell them now about all this big news. Soon they start to blame me for everything and say I come to Harare North to sponge off Shingi, cause havoc in his life and now look what happen?

There is letter for Shingi. It's from home. I take it to my room and open it. It's from some uncle who is rural farmer that the government have resettle with dozens of other families on some farm in Triangle district. He wonder if Shingi can send him only one Land Rover Defender as it will go long way towards helping with carrying things at the farm because right now his one-year-old likkle girl don't even have food to eat.

What kind of style is this? Straight and square, I write back warning uncle to 'stop embarrassing yourself. You know what the reaction of m'learned friends in Parliament will be if I start sending them Her Majesty's Land Rover Defenders to my tribesman, don't you? Even if I am careful, Land Rover Defender is not something that you can thief and put inside your pocket like mango, is it?'

But after I remember that he have got likkle hungry girl I think of Tsitsi's baby; I send him £100 for the small girl. Why people always use small children to make you feel like maggots is eating you inside, I don't get the score.

27

I wander through them streets of Brixton, Stockwell, Oval and Kennington, idly kicking them empty fizzy drink cans around, and allow things to bleed out of my head. His east London relatives, they call again. I don't answer. I'm not ready. If Shingi have tell them that I was Green Bomber and I tell them what happen now, soon they cause big problems for me and all that kind of style.

I get home and another letter have land from some gold-panning uncle who want Shingi to invest £5,000 in his gold-panning project. He is sure this is good investment that will birth US$100,000 per year. He wait at Shingi's mother's house for reply.

Now I can sniff sniff that the whole of Shingi's clan have come together to celebrate Shingi Parliament graft. Them old villagers, grumpy goat traders from the outbacks, and them 200-year-old grandmothers have maybe gather at MaiShingi's house. Even though she's not his real mother.

This kind of thing meant to be deal with by Shingi now look.

I write and remind this uncle that gold-panning is illegal and urge him to consider what kind of example he give to his small children by ruining them our riverbanks and filling rivers with poison chemicals. 'Also pass the message to everyone who is there that I have big doubt that Mother need the company of them people who have nothing to do except to sit all day fishing for food in every one of she smiles,' I tell him.

I kick myself because I have post that letter because I am worryful. That uncle, what is he going to think of Shingi now? When morning come I have to wire him £100 to keep him sweet or otherwise he take it out on Shingi.

28

I sleep. I wake up. Me I sleep. I see Shingi in one dream. I wake up. I sleep.

This Shingi thing now sit tight inside me. I also have to catch some graft soon.

I catch bus again to go look for graft. I have not eat none of the porridge or steak that I have cook yesterday because there's heaps of worry inside my head.

Once on the bus me I squeeze into the corner and I see my face reflect on the window. It is clenched tight like old demon's. I look down on floor; I am frightened I will see ghost of Shingi looking back.

I get back home and now there's letter from MaiShingi; she is telling me about tragedy that nearly befall them. To celebrate Shingi's success in Parliament, she buy she husband's father big bokkle of the old brandy. He have also hobble into she house from nowhere. While sitting under the peach tree at the back of house without no supervision, the old native down the 750ml bokkle in less than one hour, stumble into kitchen dribbling, frightening woman and small children, mumble and pass out. He get revive in hospital where he spend the week recovering.

We should thank the Lord that grandfather have survive. But please keep the news under wraps as I don't want to find myself in embarrassing position if them papers and TV people get wind of it, especially considering that I have friends in Parliament that have relatives that can handle they drink, I write back. Stupid old hen, she reply with hospital invoices, pharmacy receipts and many other vexing expenses like bus fares that is required for grandfather to head back to his home. I want to point out that she forget to add VAT to she invoices and that She Majesty's Treasury Department want she to reveal she VAT number before any payment is given, but I don't. This is Shingi's mother. I go to Western Union and wire she £100.

My trousers is dirty; in the morning me I go inside Shingi's room and borrow pair of trousers. I borrow his hat too. I go to Brixton Market. I buy two mangoes. Maybe I should go see Shingi.

You family; this has get out of hand now. Big nuisance, I want to tell him. But I run out of ginger before going to hospital.

Shingi's London relatives, they leave two messages on phone looking for Shingi. Me I don't know what they want. *Will phone you. Me I am busy*, that's the text message I send to them this time.

I get back and there's another letter from home. It's from Shingi's Uncle Sinyoro. The one that play big brother to Shingi's mother. The cat killer. Now he is writing this long letter asking why Shingi is writing stupid letters to his mother. He think that he is giving Shingi some dressing-down, you know that kind of style: yari yari yari I have big concern for you over there . . . When are you coming back home? . . . Stop this silly talk about being in Parliament . . . I will arrange for air ticket for you with Air Zimbabwe . . . he go on and on. Now, some nincompoop bureaucrat in jacket and tie, clutching sheaf of paper, is easy target to shoot down. I write to him to inform him that 'Uncle Sinyoro, me I come back home on the 44th of the month. Fill this on them your forms and tick all them correct boxes.' That drain the oil out of his head and leave him with no ginger because he never write again.

Then some old aunt of Shingi's she also drop one and start with grand kind of speech telling Shingi he have grow up into big man. Now she ask if he is able to help she keep up with them payments for funeral insurance because she think she is growing old and don't want troubling anyone if she suddenly drop dead. She say she will pay back the money and that nearly make me go kak kak kak because me I have hear this number before. Try another trick, old hen.

Downstairs Dave and Jenny is now causing racket, over what I don't know. I go down and tell them straight and square, 'I don't want to see you inside this house no more. I don't want to see nothing that belong to you. Take everything.'

My head is full of things. Shingi's family is doing pee into my porridge. MaiShingi have stretch my patience now; in the past week she have write another letter demanding money for things like java skirt, small TV, food for every clansman and his dog, the list get endless.

29

Them east London relatives have call donkey number of times now. I sit tight.

Another letter for Shingi arrive from MaiShingi. She bawl that the government have send bulldozers to demolish people's houses and they new four-room house have been demolished in second wave of Operation *Murambatsvina*. Now many people become homeless, Zimbabwe is no more she cry. Me I don't have no sympathy for Zimbabwean people about this because they have spend lot of time throwing they tails all over and trying to vote for opposition party. Now look where this have landed them. The winds is howling through house of stones, tall trees is swaying and people's lives beginning to fall apart, everything start to fall apart now and they think that me I can solve all they problems?

Me I sleep over things so I can think clear. I wake up and text message arrive from them London relatives asking why I don't call like I promise two weeks ago.

Evening. My chest is full of wriggling things now and get tight like my suitcase. I go to kitchen to eat. I cut bread. It refuse to go down throat. I spit it into sink and go back to my room.

I shut my eyes to sleep but I am wide awake. I have to wash my hands of Shingi now. I switch light on because in the dark I become more awake. The mushrooms on my ceiling is starting to grow again. I sit on my suitcase and look out of my eye into street. Nothing happening. Even shadows stop moving.

I feel sleepy. I switch light off and lie down; I am wide awake.

I turn. In the east, cold old sun start to climb up over them jagged roof and jutting chimneys throw shadows. I have to make my mind up. When I hear the bells ringing at 7am, I get out of bed, wear my twelve-pocket coat and get out of house for early-morning walk to sort my head. I want to go to the river. Everyone in London is going to they graft.

I catch Tube and find myself sitting on old bench under Waterloo Bridge; trying to reason with power; my head start to get hot. I throw my cigarette stub onto the pavement, grind it hard with my boot and step off. One more second on that bench, I will have change my mind. I have make final decision now – Shingi none of my business no more.

I head for Waterloo station with big stride.

When I climb out of Brixton Tube station, some pale icy sun hang in the sky like frozen pizza base. In them these mental streets, bitter cold wind is blowing. And the traffic lights – they is red like ketchup.

To the right of station entrance, newspaper vendors stand beside pile of copies of *Evening Standard*. On front page of every one of them papers President Robert Mugabe's face folded in two. I still can identify His Excellency. The paper say that Zimbabwe run out toilet paper.

I step into the house, shut the door, lock it and jam it with long floorboard that is lying loose, shutting out Dave and Jenny, who already have gone out. There is no heating in the house; small icicles going to be on the ceiling any minute.

Dave and Jenny come back last night and knock on the door until they give up. Me, I lie on my bed most of the day trying not to think about nothing.

I have not have shower in days because my pubic hair is maybe turning blue. I have animal odour that is always around them stressed people. Outside the city is approaching peak hour; I imagine them sounds: one computer falling off some desk in some London Underground control room and causing delays on the Victoria Line. The heavy breathing of two over-caffeinate men panicking in the control room. Inside them crowded late trains, vex passengers have desert them trains and make for the station exits where they gush out of the earth, some of them waving them caffè lattes in the air as usual and elbow others out of they way. Why them people in Harare North always refuse to take they medication me I don't get the score.

Inside my suitcase, that Moschino Parfum that I buy for Tsitsi but never have chance to give it to she, it has been leaking. It is cheap fake perfume; proper genuine things don't leak without being opened. I bin it.

I go to toilet. I reason hard. I get out of the toilet and go to lie on Shingi's bed. Shingi's pocket album is still on the floor, by his bed. It contain photo of his mother. She look like nice mother and remind me of my mother in some funny way. I get into my blankets, roll some skunk.

I wake up and realise I had fall asleep. It's maybe after four o'clock in the afternoon. But it also can be after six o'clock because from outside, the street lamp is already beaming into my room. I check Shingi's mobile phone – it say it's 3.03pm. I get out of bed, open my suitcase to take clean socks out and the smell of Mother hit my nose and make me feel dizzy. I put on my brown shoes, grab my twelve-pocket coat, and as quick as brown fox, leave the house and go down to Brixton Road to wait for bus to go to city to look for graft.

The 159 bus come and it take me straight to Bond Street station where I jump off because I have to check out for the second time that place where they stick many grafts on the window. But Shingi is still in my head, so me I go window-shopping to get him out of the head first. The city swirl around me like it is in the grip of bitter winds and it make me feel dizzy.

To get this funny feeling off my tail, me I go into West One Shopping Centre where I see electronics shop is flaunting them latest hi-fis, iPods and flat-screen TVs. I quick my pace past the shop, not wanting to let such desire catch me.

And suddenly absent-minded, I stray into clothes shop fizzing over with them people. My odour suddenly back. Over one of the mirrors to the right of the entrance, they have stick notice: **This mirror compresses your image and makes you look short, squat and wide. We suggest you go to the basement where there's a better mirror that will make you look nice.** I think it would be hard for me to tell which is normal mirror – the one downstairs or the one that I am looking at – but me I see no point in wasting time on this.

I throw my eye into basement and down there is this short customer queue of them beautiful women with them fibreglass fingernail and tattoo above they tail-bones. It is inching forward to the till. The sight is powerful and maybe untie spaghetti jumble of them questions inside my head, but which have been answered and which not, I have no way of tell. I stagger out of the shop like I am emerging from big battle.

207

30

Where are you? Back later, that's the note Dave leave on the door. I open the door, step in, lock it and jam it again.

I walk into kitchen and Shingi's fat rat rumble across them floorboards like big marble and disappear into some hole on the floorboards. I ignore the rat, grab plastic cup from the sink and wash it. The sink drain do one belch and bad stench shoot up and hang in the air. In house across the road the curtain twitch, but I don't care one bag of beans. In the next house members of Romanian family is crowded at they windows again: mother, two teenage sons, younger daughter and maybe the mother's sister. The whole tribe. But today I stand my ground, whip them with powerful look and they scatter away from the windows and leave me to drink my water before I am tossing the cup into the sink bowl and stepping off.

I sleep with the screwdriver under my pillow. I am alone now since Jenny and Dave go. I sleep in my clothes and shoes because I have make big vow never to allow any intruder to set they eyes on me without my clothes on. If you is taken by surprise, once your enemy see you in them shabby underpants, the humiliation is big; you is two times set back and is fighting from position of big disadvantage.

In the morning I am lying on my bed and I hear voice saying, '. . . we could try the kitchen window.' I know straight away that someone need to be deal with quick.

I grab the screwdriver, kick the blankets off me and step down-stairs. Holding the screwdriver tight, I fling the front door open. There, looking wretched like Israelites that have walk all the way from Egypt, is Dave and Jenny. I have been too optimistic to think that they is not coming back again. The winds is now blowing in different direction but they don't get it. Now they is pushing back again.

Hanging around Dave's neck and almost toppling him to the ground is the binoculars that he get from the Salvation Army shop and now use for trying to check time off the Big Ben in Westminster while sitting under the chestnut tree in Brixton.

They have just been to Marks & Spencer's bins again. There's bag of tinned food and sandwiches hanging on Dave's microscooter. From behind his gap tooth and disorderly beard, Dave look at my hand with horror, but Jenny is not bothered. She scruffy dog wag tail, while she mouse have nose peeping out of she jacket's side pocket. Jenny have big stain on she jeans that run down she right leg all the way into one of she para-military boots.

I show them my teethies in good friendly way – 'You people give me big fright, I was expect them burglars.'

Dave is silent; the wart on his nose throb and start to get fiery red. I know he think that I'm spinning him the fat old jazz number. His eyes shine and fill with vex. I don't know how to continue from there; I shut door and go back inside house and sit on the stair. As they walk away I hear the tinkle tinkle of them likkle bells that Jenny always keep tied to she boots.

In the afternoon, I jump out of my bed, gather all of Dave and Jenny's belongings – cigarette lighters, Rizlas, blankets and syringes – and throw them out. I don't know what to do with Shingi's belongings. He have few more things than Dave and

Jenny. It is not his things inside the house that is bother me, but those that he have accumulate in the back garden, those that he fish them out of skips. Computer monitors, surge protectors, toasters, CDs and bathroom accessories, they is all piled up in the garden. Three TV sets is stack on each each. The rest of them items, Shingi arrange around the TV sets according to they importance to him.

Days leap quick and die on the horizon. Every night I come back from graft hunting and, for long time, gaze at Shingi's things. I can't make decision and his things is making frightful silence with each day that pass. I am also worryful about *mamhepo*. I am worryful because Shingi's mother originally come from Chipinge near Banda. But I observe moment of silence in the garden and after that I busy myself carrying all of Shingi's things to the pavement outside, where I stack them up for passers-by to help themselves. The Romanian family have learn to do the curtain-twitching thing, I can tell.

I have move all of Shingi's things. I go into the kitchen, cut two thick slices of bread, butter them thickly, pour some Coke and go upstairs to my room where I slide into them my blankets and feast hard.

Then I get my cigarette out and set it on fire. It crackle and glow in front of my face and make me feel like I am in Mother's womb, safe and feeling good.

This Comrade Mhiripiri jazz number have so nearly push me over the edge. No wonder why I sometimes find myself being charmed and put under spell by my own *kaka* as it whirl about in the WC before disappearing. That has never been me.

Me I puff and reason hard.

210

31

Jenny come to invite me to poetry evening that is to be held in Clapham in memory of whale that have die after getting lost and wandering up Thames River some few weeks ago.

'In memory of whale?'

She say there will be heap of nice people but me I keep quiet because this is getting my head out of gear. She ask if I have poems about fish.

'No. If anyone hear that I have go to evening in memory of dead fish they will start to worry that something is going funny inside my head.'

Now she start telling me that she have get good news; she have decide to stop doing smack and have just have HIV test because she have been sharing too many needles with them many people. She have pass the test, she tell me.

'The results say I'm HIV-negative,' she shout with big crazy smile on she face.

'You can't tell me about HIV, I know, me I've been there in prison. I know all about it because me I have had bicycle spoke being hold close to my heart by some thug that give me no choice. And they do the HIV test on everyone before they leave prison. And my result, it come out bad, me I know.' I shut the door on she face. She's lunatic, Jenny. HIV-negative; how can negative be good news?

You see it in the faces of the health people that hand the paper to you when you leave prison. They don't say no word. One of them maybe stand leaning against desk with one hand on hip looking at you like you is already dead thing. That's because they know that everyone in prison have HIV. They eyes is talking, you can tell and you even hear them whisper as you leave they room because they know you have it. When you open your envelope, the result is on the paper. HIV-negative, that's what it say. Who has ever hear of good news that is negative?

Negative result. But you don't throw it away. It's proof that life is not fair. You keep it inside the pocket. You keep it inside the suitcase where no one can see it. Right there. Life is not fair, you even tell that traitor in Goromonzi when you give him your touch because you was knowing that tomorrow you is going to be dead. And it's all because life is never fair, you tell him, but he don't understand you is also dying and it's not your fault. By the end he can only tell you apart from everyone because of your touch; the skill and the laughter. Jenny cannot be right, otherwise everything has been one big waste. Life is not fair, me I know.

I follow Jenny out to chestnut tree. She get my head all out of gear.

Under the tree is Dave. He start shouting: yeee you thief my ideas; you have to give back my notebook that I leave in your house.

He shout and stagger all over. Me I sit down, cough, move the phlegm out of my lungs and spit on the ground.

'Thief; fuckin' thief, give me my notebook,' Dave keep bawling.

I clear my throat. I spit on the ground. Close to his boot.

Now he start silly style: yeee do you want to fight me, do you want to fight me? You call all your boys and I call mine then we will see; my boys going to kill ya two-faced Donald Duck yari yari yari!

'No fighting here,' someone say but Dave don't stop. He is throwing them arms in the air in that kind of style.

212

The tall man with them soldier's eyes that I once see at Elser Cafe now come and try to pull Dave away but Dave have make up his mind that he don't like my guts and won't move. I step back to our house.

32

I get home and I find there is another letter from Shingi's uncle, Sinyoro the old nincompoop. He is worried that Shingi have lose his head or something. He make big threat of coming to London. I bin the letter.

The kitchen-sink bowl is nearly overflow with things floating on water. There is no movement down the sink drain, and stench is starting to become hard to live with. The cupboard door below the sink have long fall off hinges, and after being toss about, soak with spilt water, and trampled on, it have lost its colour and have expand, warp and crack. It lean against the cupboard frame.

I lift the door and place it flat on the floor.

From the rubber P-trap, which have swell and is covered by fungus, water drip down onto the floor of the cupboard, which have also start to rot; there's heaps of bread that Shingi have been putting there to feed the rat. Now mushrooms is growing everywhere.

I go down on my knees for closer look. Scatterings of *kaka* by Shingi's rat is fertilising mushrooms on the floor of cupboard. Rat is dangerous thing inside house. He can eat anything – plastic, wire, bread or wood. This is danger to my suitcase; people going to laugh if they hear that my suitcase and money for my plane ticket get eat by some rat.

I take plastic bag, pick the rotting bread and put it inside bin. Then I pick the cupboard door and put it back where it have been.

Everything falling apart. I don't know how to fix this. I have to stop the rat. He is hitting my food.

I go to my room and write inside my head that, from now on, I keep sharp lookout for the rat who is doing all the *kaka*.

I want to eat. I'm hungry. I go to kitchen to find bread and I find that Shingi's rat have nibble it. I go to my room and put my suitcase on windowsill; you never know what else this rat is going to eat. Then I write to them Ancient & Honourable Society of Rat Catchers. Me I give detail of everything that is about to start in the house because some of my plane ticket money is in danger of being eat now. Now I feel cold like I start to catch fever, so I wear my twelve-pocket coat and sit on floor by the window to finish writing letter.

Now I start big wait for rat in the kitchen.

It's late into night but I have no sleep. I have already miss rat once now with claw hammer that Shingi pick from skip. Even if I feel like I have fever inside my head I sit on the stair on the ground floor waiting patient holding my screwdriver and claw hammer.

The rat don't come out all night.

I come from graft hunting and there is rat *kaka* on the kitchen floor, so I don't go to graft hunting the following day.

I go to buy bread – only enough for me since I am now the only one left inside our house. I come back, there is rat's *kaka* by the stairs. I stop going out of house altogether.

I have not hear from them, the Ancient & Honourable Society of Rat Catchers. So I write another letter to them reminding them that even if I am original native, me I still know misbehaviour by professional organisation; if they cannot help at least they tell me straight and square. I don't manage to send the letter because I don't want to go out of the house and come back to find rat has do *kaka* on the floor again.

*   *   *

Inside our house. Shadows shiver, become long, become short and disappear; days scatter away like birds flying off the wire. I stop sleeping.

I walk around the house with screwdriver and claw hammer, my boots make clattering sound on them floorboards. It is the beginning of week and right under my nose the rat have do more *kaka*. But I have been keeping my eyes wide open.

I have one rat to kill or else I die in this foreign place. I have to get to source of the problem before I get overwhelmed. I sense it coming. The rat want to keep me in London now.

Tuesday night. I am almost nodding off when the rat appear at kitchen doorway. I throw spanner and catch him on his bum. He fly into the air, come down on the floorboards, try to scurry away but his behind legs look like they is broken so that he remain on the same spot like the squirrel that I kill in the park. I think I have maybe break his spine or something. When I get up to finish him off, he recover and slip into some hole that I can't fit into. But I know that I have deal fatal blow and expect the smell of rotting body in them coming days. No one is going to eat my money.

On morning Wednesday, I am in good mood. I go out to buy food. I come back to the squat and there is no rat *kaka* nowhere.

In the evening I go to the chestnut tree. No Dave, no Jenny is there. No one that I know. When I come back at night there is no rat nowhere.

Thursday morning. I wake up and there is not one rat *kaka* anywhere. I am over the moon.

Friday morning. I wake up. I expect the smell of the rotting rat, but there is no smell in the air. But I know that the body need to be in real decay before smell can start to come out of them floorboards so I relax.

Saturday morning. Still no rat droppings nowhere. Also no smell.

Sunday morning. I am scared stiff. I drink one litre of Coca-Cola and try to relax for the rest of the morning. Then the diarrhoea start and I know for sure Jenny was wrong because how can you have diarrhoea if you don't have no Aids? And the rat, maybe he have not die. He is recovering somewhere under them floorboards of my squat.

Sunday evening. I reason up some way of finding out what happen to the rat.

I can take them kitchen cupboards apart; maybe rat is at the bottom? Or I can rip open them floorboards in the kitchen.

Midnight. I throw myself into this graft. I start to rip them kitchen-floor skirting out with claw hammer. Then the floorboards; they pile up in the hallway. One floorboard out; I see them dusty and PVC pipes. Another floorboard, another pile of rat *kaka*, but no rat. Another litre of Coca-Cola I drink in thirty seconds.

I start to apply myself flat out on my graft. Then the diarrhoea, it come again. Even my hair now feel like cat's hair but me I know life is not fair; I don't worry; I am hard.

I don't know what time it is, but it is way after midnight when the prepay electricity meter run out of credit and suddenly there is darkness inside Shingi's head.

I can't call the whole thing off. Not now. I grope around in the darkness and them splinters of timber lodge into my fingers. I trip, fall, but get up again. My eyes now get used to the darkness. I am breathing hard; hot air is coming out of my mouth and nose. I breathe black bitter wind into our house.

I don't know for how long I work, removing all them floorboards, but soon time stop; the sun come up, come down and come up again I don't know how many times. I don't go out until this graft is done. I smoke cigarettes and fire myself up with bread. I sleep and wake up sweating because I have been having nightmare about rat eating up all my money.

I go check the money and find it is still there. But the smell of Mother have already come out of the suitcase. Now it fill the whole house.

I spend the night slamming them doors everywhere trying to frighten the rat to come out from under remaining floorboards. But I have to stop this because the crusty neighbour that shout at Jenny over dog *kaka* come to complain that I am disturbing his sleep. It is wasted night because I don't get much done.

The following evening, I have work with no disturbance. Now I go out for walk around the block. I want fresh air.

I come back to house and suddenly Shingi's mobile phone start causing one big racket on them floorboards. It's them London relatives. But this time I have no fear on my tail so I answer it.

'Shingi?'

'It's not Shingi.'

On the other end is cousin of Shingi. But that is not the scandal. The scandal is that he hand the phone to someone, and it's the old nincompoop Sinyoro. He have land in London to claim Shingi now.

Before I have even have chance to think straight, the nincompoop jump into one of those long-winded traditional greetings that go on and on and make it impossible for you to talk honestly to each each. My whole body start to ache with effort of my patience while he talk. Suddenly I decide I have to end this and I straight away ask him what he want.

'Time is everything in Harare North, you don't just call someone like you is back home and just talk talk talk without purpose. Get to the point,' I tell him. That shake him out of his style. That's when he start this big talk asking me where is my manners and why I talk like some child that was born when them village elders have gone away for beer orgy. I hang up and switch phone off.

At night I work hard. I remove them floorboards and only stop when I notice that the waters have start to lap at my ankles; I must have damage one of them pipes while removing the floorboards. Me I sit on big pile of floorboards and take rest.

Some big bell gong inside my head and suddenly I realise that maybe Shingi's relatives know our address. You don't want to hear door knock and open door only to find the nincompoop, Shingi's mother, and all them other crusty members of clan. I jump up and make my way through them piles of floorboards and go upstairs into my room where I pack my suitcase full, lift it onto my head, walk out of our house and slam the door.

33

I go to the i-Joint, some round-the-clock Internet cafe on Brixton Station Road. For £3, you stay there until 7am.

Shingi's email password is poor – originalnative. It take three tries to crack it. Inside there is only one message from Chamu; he is wondering if Shingi can send him 'a sound system' because he want to start DJing at community hall. Me I tell him to *'pull your tongue out of my bum; I have no more ginger to keep pushing away tongues that continue to stretch out for my bum and trying to thief they way into my plane ticket money. Also you is sell-out opposition supporter,'* I tell him straight and square.

I don't stay at the i-Joint too long because the guy behind the counter look at me funny and the place feel funny with only one other man that twitch every two seconds.

I carry my suitcase along Brixton Station Road, into the dark and unlit Popes Road, and find my way through them deserted market stalls on Electric Avenue where I take suitcase off my head and stop to pee on pile of garbage that spill out of industrial bins behind Boots chemist. I am halfway through my pee and the man with them soldier's eyes rumble out of the rubbish and give me big fright. Me I call for peace; I don't want to make enemies on first day out on the street. Especially after what have happen to Shingi. One flash of some ten-pence blade, one flick of tramp's wrist and one not so quick leap backward on your part and before you know it you is struggling to stop gallons of life from leaving your body. Them mental backstreets is full of death dealers.

The man with soldier's eyes is high on brew but he accept that I am sorry and we part in civil way. I go to sit under the chestnut tree. It is dark and the place is desert, but it is near sunrise because it is not long before it start getting light giving me some view of Brixton that I have never see before. Dawn come and the sun's rays start to climb across the quiet walls of them tall council estate tower blocks in the distance. Brixton Road show sweep of old street lamps that I have never see because such things can hide in daytime clamour of preachers throwing word of God at you through megaphone, cars and buses, posters, graffiti and them trains cluttering above your head as they pass over them bridges.

I fix my eyes on the bus stop outside KFC and soon start to see them figures cross them streets for some while before they is replaced by flickering commuters. Down Coldharbour Lane shops open; shutters – red, blue, green and silver – get rolled up. Some funeral procession with them clopping horses, jazz band in white uniform march past and make me think of Shingi.

34

The mobile phone start to ring again. I answer and it's Shingi's cousin again. This time he make sure he don't hand the phone to the nincompoop. I tell him that me I don't think that Shingi want to be found. That's it. Unless they want to repay the £500 that I have spend on Shingi's family?

He talk nice.

'Can we meet?'

'OK; I wait outside Brixton station as long as you come on your own, without the nincompoop or anyone else.'

By the time our phone conversation end I am in the chatter of them chestnut-tree people who is already out for the warmth of the sun. I pick my suitcase, lift it onto my head and go to Elser Cafe where I buy myself cup of tea. When the waitress bring it, the tea is too hot, so me I start to fan it with Shingi's hat. One woman carrying she baby come to sit at the table near me, but suddenly move to another table because our eyes have clash.

I finish my tea and go.

35

It is 10.49am. We is supposed to meet at eleven o'clock. I go and sit across the road from the station. When Shingi's cousin come out he is not only late by five minutes, but he also bring with him the nincompoop. He come out of the station with him, and then he leave him by newspaper vendor and go to stand alone by flower vendor where he take his mobile phone out and call me. I add two and three and figure things out.

'You is five minutes late. I can't meet you now because me I have meeting in city and have to go straight away. If you want to see me again, we meet at Bond Street station at 3pm sharp. No foolishness. And my price go up to £1,500 because me I know I have Aids. Soon I will be dead, so I also want money to buy good coffin so that I can be lay to rest close to Mother,' I tell him and hang up and switch the phone off. I watch him having bad-tempered talk with the nincompoop and they disappear into the station.

I get up, take walk down Electric Avenue. Life is not fair. Them stalls is now piled high with yams, salt fish, chicken, fruit and vegetables as the market roar back to life. I cross Atlantic Road and go to the other end of the market on Popes Road.

Jenny can't be right.

I go to the chestnut tree. I go to the Tube station and watch people but I grow tired and go through the market again. I rest at Elser Cafe because my neck is getting tired of carrying suitcase. I go to Tesco but don't buy nothing. I go to the Salvation Army shop looking for binoculars but they say they don't have any. Me I stand outside KFC. I go to the train station and sit on the bench, but them trains making noise and putting ideas into my head so me I go back to the chestnut tree.

How can HIV-negative be good news? What school did she go to, Jenny? I don't even want to waste time asking Sekai what HIV-negative mean. I'm tired of wrong answers.

No one want to talk to me and they all giving me the wide berth. And comrade commander is not there.

I touch my hair; it feel like cat's hair. Jenny cannot be right; the world is never fair, me I know. Now I even feel the diarrhoea coming but I hold it. Soon I get bored and decide to go into Brixton Tate Library. I want to read hard until smoke lift off them pages of books. I have not read properly in long time and this is the first time that I find myself with spare time to read. I want to read Sherlock Holmes.

I try to go inside the library but I am stopped by the security man; he don't like my suitcase. I try to explain to him and he start pushing me out, saying they don't want disruptive people in the library. Another important library official gang up on me but he leave at dog speed when I ask him if he can see what is pointing at him. He only start waving his fat finger from safety of staircase.

36

It is 2.37pm. I send text to Shingi's cousin and tell him I am sorry we have to cancel our meeting because I have many things to do but we can meet at Bond Street station same time tomorrow.

The sun leap up; sometimes. The sun fall down; sometimes. I visit Sherlock Holmes Museum on Baker Street. I pay good money to see Sherlock Holmes's armchair – his bedroom, magnifying glass, pipe, violin and all. Our tour guide now tell us that Sherlock Holmes is just some fiction character. Without batting one eye? I pick my suitcase and leave. What else is big con here?

I visit that shop that have the mirror that can make you look tall, beautiful and rich. I go to the basement, with my suitcase, while them shop assistants look at me in that usual London way when them people think you is in the wrong place but don't tell you straight and square. But me I don't care what civilians think.

I put suitcase down, stand in front of the mirror. I nearly suffer skin failure from lot of gooseflesh: there in front of me, the original native flash on the mirror for one second. This is the works of Banda the Chipinge wizard straight and square. I pick my suitcase and leave.

It is nearly time to meet Shingi's cousin but me I don't want to stay anywhere near Bond Street no more. I walk towards Oxford Street. I am in vigilant mood and not walking on them pavements, but right in the middle of the streets, on the white line, with

225

suitcase on my head while traffic flowing past me in different direction. That way I stay well clear of any tall building; if some dunderhead drop £1 coin from some tall building it can hit ground at 400 metres per second. If that hit your head, it feel like someone smashing into it with pickaxe while you is strolling absent-minded on the street. We have talk about it before with Dave and Shingi.

I walk on the white line with suitcase on my head. Nothing can hit my head. I feeling like *umgodoyi* – the homeless dog that roam them villages scavenging until brave villager relieve it of its misery by hit its head with rock. *Umgodoyi* have no home like the winds. That's why *umgodoyi*'s soul is tear from his body in rough way. That's what everyone want to do to me, me I know.

I stop and call Shingi's cousin and tell him where I am if he want to find me.

'You also have to be careful and look out for coins that might hit your head because them tall buildings is full of dunderheads in they smart suits.' But he is too late coming. I have to ride number 3 bus to Brixton. I call him to say that he should learn to keep time.

'This is Harare North, you forget? Now, if you still want to see me let's meet in Brixton. Come with US$5,000 because me I also have to buy pills for HIV soon. Life is not fair, you know.'

37

When Shingi's cousin arrive in Brixton he call me again and I ask him how much money he is bringing. He fail to answer me so, with sweet politeness, I ask him to go think again and call me with nice number; even if you is homeboy it don't mean I can let your family mess up my money and you don't pay nothing. When he call again me I ask him, what is the number that you have now decide is good for me? Now he sigh and just go all cheap and stupid on me. He hesitate, stammer but finally mention the right number. US$5,000.

'We meet inside Shingi's head,' I tell him and he sound lost again. 'The house!' I have to give him clue. Then there is too many voices on the phone, they start to get mix up and it is hard to tell which voice is which, let alone what or which question to answer. I hang up.

Before long it is after midnight and I am pacing up and down deserted Atlantic Road, empty of all them market vendors. The sky get dark with them fat mama clouds and hide the moon and some strong wind suddenly come and blow Shingi's hat off my head, take it high into the air and it land on the train bridge above me. I have no ginger to go after the hat and so I go on to Electric Lane hoping to find the man with them soldier's eyes. I want to pee on someone. Then I notice that because I forget to lock it, my suitcase have break open and the things inside have unravel and scatter all over them streets and get lost. Even the proof; my test result. It's gone. Nothing is left inside suitcase except the smell of Mother.

I put the suitcase down on the pavement to check again what have happen; it's full of nothing.

38

Soft rain start and get the tarmac wet so that them street lamps reflect off the wet tarmac doubling up in numbers. Even me – there is my double image reflected on the wet tarmac. In the sky the moon struggle to come out of them clouds. Shingi's trousers is missing now, I am only in his underpants. Right in front of my feeties there is puddle of water that has form from the rain and street lamp is shining into it. I look down into puddle; the crack that is screaming out of corner of my glasses' left lens in all directions make things unclear; I can see Shingi looking straight back. My stump finger now feel cold and sore from carrying suitcase. I shake my head and Shingi shake his head until I start to feel dizzy. Why he want to shake me out of his head like so, me I don't know.

I take few steps following Shingi's nose in no particular direction. I run. I can feel my bum jump jump behind me like heap of jelly. I stop. Paul and Uncle Sinyoro have give up calling now; they fail to raise the money. But you can't trust them; maybe they is now chasing you with them big rocks in they hands wanting to punish you like you are *umgodoyi*. Forgiveness is the best kind of punishment. You don't know when or from which direction the rock of truth will come tearing through the air to smash your head and bring everything to one final end.

Half naked, you turn left into Electric Avenue and walk. You start to hear in tongues; it feel like Shingi is on his way back to life. You can tell, you know it; Shingi is now coming back. Already there's struggle over your feeties; you are telling right foot to go in one direction and he is telling left foot to go in another direction. You tell the right foot to go in one direction and he is being traitor shoe-doctor and tell left foot to go in another direction. You stand there in them mental backstreets and one big battle rage even if you have no more ginger for it.

Acknowledgements

Special thanks to the following people who helped make this book a reality: Jackie Batanda, Tom Bullough, Kate Howell, Delia Jarrett-Macauley, Parselelo Kantai, Monica Arac De Nyeko, Chika Unigwe, Charlie Ward and most of all Ellah Allfrey, Kevin Conroy-Scott and Poet Hank.